Bogus AZZ Hood Chick

By: PattiCake Taylor

A (Pa Pow Boom Kack Productions)

A urban Fiction Novel

Bogus Azz Hood Chick/ PattiCake Taylor

This book is a work of fiction. Names, characters, places and incidents either are products of the author's imagination or are used fictitiously any resemblance to actual events, locations or persons, living or dead are entirely coincidental.

Proof read by: Tammy G. & Bo$$~Lady (Tonya)

Copyrighted © 2006 Revised 2012 by PattiCake Taylor

Slightly revised by PattiCake Taylor Jan 2015

ISBN-13: 978-1481884587

ISBN-10: 1481884587

Bogus Azz Hood Chick/ PattiCake Taylor

Dreams DO Come TRUE!!!!

I PattiCake Taylor had no professional help during this process, so YES, I did that by myself even if you see a few bumps & humps as you read… This NOVEL is da shit.. lol

P.S If you purchase this after the 1st of the year 2015 I have made a few slight changes… thank you so much for all your support… BAM

Bogus Azz Hood Chick/ PattiCake Taylor

Ms. PattiCake Taylor was born and raised in Chicago Illinois, with a dream to have stardom and success some way. This is PattiCake Taylor 1st Novel. She appeared on Various Talk shows and Radio. PattiCake has also appeared in a couple of movie's and a web series in hopes of becoming an actress, or having her own talk show or even reality show.

PattiCake has one beautiful daughter in college. She still resides in the windy city Chicago. She enjoys riding motorcycles, reading, traveling, meeting new people, and life as a whole.

You can reach her via email PattiCake@PaPowBoomKack.com or PattiCakeTaylor@Yahoo.com

Facebook.com/PattiCake613 please send a message with your request.

@PattiCake33 on Twitter

PattiCake T << is her LIKE/Fan page on FaceBook

PattiCake613 on Instagram

All fan mail can be sent to: PattiCake Taylor, P.O box 3326 Oak Park IL, 60603

ORDER your NOVEL: **Amazon.com**

Bogus Azz Hood Chick/ PattiCake Taylor

PattiCake's Movie Guest Appearances…..

Guest appearance in: The lies we tell but the secrets we keep movie part 2 & 3 by Milon V. Parker as "PEACHES" my 1st movie, Thank you so much… xoxo… get your movies, books & etc by Milon V. Parker www.ThemakingsofMVP.com

Guest appearance in: If I was your girl Web-Series by Coquie Hughes as "Dr. Patti Jones" Thank U so much

Guest appearance in: Life under the Rainbow movie by Kristie Turner as "Myself" Thank U so much "The Turners"

Guest appearance in: Vulture City 2 as "Myself" Thank you so much Marcus Carothers

Bogus Azz Hood Chick/ PattiCake Taylor

Words from PattiCake....

My 1st fiction Novel.... WOW, it took a minute in the making but it's my time now. I'm bless & thankful.

I really wanted to write a book about me & my life but then I got this boring job. I got my 1st taste of Fiction, thanks to Patricia Shug Hobson, she told me about a book called The Coldest Winter Ever by Sister Souljah.

So I decided to write a fiction novel. I wanted excitement, a page turner & a jaw dropper so here it is, BOGUS AZZ HOOD CHICK!

In closing once again I just want to say THANKS a million, thanks for supporting me, my new fans and old fans, Thanks for saying yes to PattiCake!!

Bogus Azz Hood Chick/ PattiCake Taylor

Acknowledgements/ Shout outs!!!!!

To my peeps on lock down: Be encouraged:

Mario (Rio), my 1st love, all I'm gonna say is The Skating Rink on 87th street, 1991.. Lmao it was on & popping! Keep your head up, stay focus, and thank you for always being positive even through your situation. You will hit the land soon. I LOVE YOU… always & 4Ever no matter what!! You know what it is…. Muah! xoxo

Ronnie Baby, Smile, it's almost over. You've been doing well in spite of, keep your head up, and know Granny Knox & I got your back. Love ya xoxo

Monica!! Hey Boo Boo stank…. Lol, I love you always… I will never forget those who were there for me. Stay positive and know that God answers prayers in due time.

Cynica … Smile Cyn city!! xoxo! See you soon!! I love you!!

Hey Jay… Keep your head up & continue to praise god as you do. I wish you the best & I love you.

Nita, hey love…. we will always be sister's I love you, be encourage.

D.R.T, I bet you thought I forgot about you but I didn't!! I'm still waiting on my trip to New Orleans, it's about to go down!! love ya!

Bogus Azz Hood Chick/ PattiCake Taylor

I just want to say THANK YOU to everyone, Family, Friends, FANS, & Haters too {lol} I love you.

Loving ALL my family, I love you mom & my Auntie Rose who always said YES to me, always had Patti's back, Thank you & I love you!

To: my one & only momma proud of you, "Shavia a.k.a Shab"

My Best friends for over 15 years: Tammy Robinson ~ Gant, Tonya Bo$$~Lady Brown, Nicole Nikki King, & Rodney Cooper.. xoxo & I love YOU!!

The SEARS family & FAMILY, I loooooooove you… momma Mae muah!

R.I.P auntie Pamela Taylor I miss ya "DOMESTIC Violence" is never okay.

Cousin John D. Evans (The Evans Poetry Collection)… Thanks 4 always pushing & asking are you gonna finish your book!! I wish you much more success! Xoxo

Much love with plenty of hugs to my Chocolate Drop " I am da ONE" By Fresh… who most deafly stay fresh… BAM "Fresh Kid"

Bogus Azz Hood Chick/ PattiCake Taylor

LASTLY: Shout outs oh yeah "Pa Pow BOOM Kack "KACK" dot BAM" Bionce Foxx, Ms. Foxx on the box. Thank you for letting me hit them air waves with you, when you were a WGCI/107.5 Personality. I will never 4get Feb 3, 2003 BAM!!

Ellis E~Money thanks 4 the support during those long night shifts at work 2006, geesh! Lol…even though I didn't finish then, I'M FINISHED NOW!!

Natalie McNeal, Dannie Seals, N.V~Me social club, << much love 2 you, I heart you!! Hey GRU too many names 2 mention but Thank U, Kack, kack MUAH dot BAM!!

Gary Heyward author of Correction Officer, thank you for taking my call, I wish you much more success.

To the: Taylor, Stokes, White, Young, Ward, Hollins, Cooper,

Rogers, Johnson, Jackson, Bailey, Williams, Price, McToy,

King, Robinson, Lee, & Hurd Family … MUAH!! Love ya!

Thanks to my Cover model: who I meet in New York 2011 on The Bill Cunningham show: who happen to have the same name (Cola) as my character in my Novel: Cola Fox >> www.ColaFox.com

Sarah Gary: Thank You for the wonderful art work, I added them to my website: Sarah's contact info: If you want a drawing. http://www.facebook.com/sarah.queeninkfulthoughts

Bogus Azz Hood Chick/ PattiCake Taylor 2

Cola Krown Blue Royalty Johnson,

A given name by her Alcoholic mother Marlene who always seemed to have a cup of Cola and Krown Blue Royal in her hand!

Cola is only eleven years old. She's fast and out of control, seeking the attention of her Alcoholic mother Marlene, despite having a good home with her grandmother Lynda B. After endless times of stealing and running away, Grandma Lynda B gets tired and fed up she warns Cola to do better or else. Cola, letting her grandmother's words go in one ear and out the other because she had heard it all before and she's gonna do what the hell she wants. It's CKBRJ way or no way!

BUT THEN…… Cola gets the wake up call of her life. She's ready to kill, steal & destroy anything or anyone that stands in her way! Bi-Polar should have been her middle name.

Bogus Azz Hood Chick/ PattiCake Taylor 3

Hey WaVon, Cola said so sexy made him do a double take. "girl" what the hell you doing out at 11:00 at night, don't you got school in the morning? WaVon said. Cola smile "yeah AND your point".

"My point is your only eleven years old and your ass should be in the house" he said. "Whatever" Cola said, "anyway my Grandma think I'm at a friend house". "Well take your ass to your friend house and get your fast ass off the corner" replied WaVon.

Cola waited a few minutes and smiled again. "Why in the hell you standing there smiling" WaVon asked? "I'm waiting on my friend" Cola stated. "Where she at then" WaVon said with a slight attitude. "Who said it was a she, how you know it's not a HE" Cola snap back.

Cola was waiting on her friend Gummy, she was 3 years older then Cola and boy crazy, all the boys called her Gummy because she didn't have no teeth. Sadly Gummy was in a bad car accident, and it caused her to lose all her grill.

Bogus Azz Hood Chick/ PattiCake Taylor 4

Gummy was waiting on her new teeth to be made, word on the street was that she could suck a mean dick.

Gummy was only 14 years old! "Cola", COLA yelled WaVon! "What gat damn it, you are wearing my fucking name out WaVooooooon" Cola said. "Take your fast ass home NOW before you get busted for curfew" WaVon said". Cola smile wide and bright and said let's go then! "Let's go" WaVon said, "get your ass out of here, your ass is jail bait". "No thank you ma". Cola started laughing, "nigga I see the way you be looking at me".

"Hold on shorty" Wavon said, "What the fuck can I do with you"? "I'm muther fucking eighteen years old and your ass is eleven, you do the fucking math" he said. "You young and acting real stupid right now" Wavon said. "OH I'm acting stupid huh"! "aiight check this" Cola said, "I'm going to walk to the corner and if you don't want my company tonight you won't follow me". WaVon looked Cola up and down, she was filled out real thick, WaVon couldn't help but to lick his lips, and think of how tight that virgin pussy would be. Cola got half way down the block when Wavon came running up behind her saying aiight shorty let's go to my crib and watch television.

Cola followed WaVon home. He had this little hole in the wall studio apartment on the westside of Chicago with a whole lot of roaches, a small 13inch black and white television, and a twin size bed that was on the floor. After being in the crib for about fifteen minutes WaVon started talking crazy to Cola about her being fast and every time he saw her some little punk ass nigga was in her face. "You need to stop hanging with these older girls Cola, you too advance for your age" WaVon said "Well I can't help that I'm cute and got a nice body, I see it for show pulled you, and why you think my momma name me Cola because she knew I would have a cola shape just like her" Cola said.

WaVon said "YES... Indeed", as his mind drifted wondering how an eleven year old could have a body as if she was eighteen and had one of those big midget booties only Cola wasn't a midget. "EXCUSE me" Cola said, what you just say WaVon? "nothing girl" he shouted! laughing at himself, "you want some grape kool-aid"? "Hell nawl nigga I see them roaches crawling around" Cola answered with a laugh.

"Fuck you man", WaVon said. "I put down roach spray and they seem to eat it instead of dying from it".

Cola and WaVon was just sitting there and all the sudden WaVon reached over and kissed Cola. After five minutes or so WaVon started doing things to Cola he knew he could go to jail for, but being a man he was thinking with the wrong head.

WaVon busted out and said, "do you want to be my little secret?" "You know I'm too old for you". Cola was like okay I'll be your little secret WaVon but don't hurt my feelings. As WaVon kissed Cola, he mouthed I love you baby, I love Cola! "Hold up nigga" Cola said, "you know your ass don't love me stop lying". "Yes I do" WaVon said "let me show you". WaVon then started removing Cola's clothes and started

Bogus Azz Hood Chick/ PattiCake Taylor 7

kissing her mouth full of titties, all while removing his clothes. WaVon was too thirsty to get into her panties. He was going to have sex with a virgin and he didn't care that she was only eleven years old. Pussy didn't have an age or face as far as he was concerned.

At first Cola wanted him to stop but this was what was happening. All the other girls was talking about sex and Cola wanted to know what the deal was because no adult really talked to their children about sex in the eighties. Children were supposed to know better.

WaVon humped on Cola all night and when daylight came he put her out of his apartment saying remember we are a secret. Cola waved her hand and said whatever boy. Cola wasn't feeling good, she could barely walk and she was bleeding real bad. Cola went home, she was living with her grandma Lynda B at the time. Cola had been living on and off with her mom and grandma, because Marlene, Cola's mother was twenty six years old and loved running the streets. She loved drinking, smoking weed and whatever else a party consisted of.

   Grandma Lynda was heated at Cola. Gummy mother had called looking for her so grandma Lynda knew Cola had lied about being at Gummy's house. Lynda got out her belt and beat the black off Cola Krown Blue Royalty Johnson as soon as she walk through the door.

   Cola Krown Blue Royalty was Cola's real name. Marlene's favorite drink was Cola and Krown Blue Royal on the rocks, and when she went into labor that's exactly what Marlene was drinking. After the beating Cola now had a sore ass and box cake, her box cake was her private area. Cola took a long bath. She had to try and feel better before going to school.

   Cola knew she would have a better day at school. It was Friday and she was the school bully and everybody was scared of her because she had a mouth of power. The kids at school gave her money, shoes, clothes and even their lunches if they had to! Cola could fight her ass off which is why everyone was scared of her. She had proven that one summer day when she beat the brakes off Nicole. Nicole thought Cola was scared of her and couldn't fight because her mom told her anyone with that much mouth be wolfing. Nicole took what her mother told her and ran with it. Nicole went home with two black eyes and a busted lip that day.

It was the weekend and Cola wanted to go outside with the kids to play double dutch. Cola sang D-I-S-H, D for Double Dutch. I for Irish, S for Single and H for Hop. Cola was on punishment and she couldn't go outside for the whole weekend.

On Monday Cola didn't want to go to school so she asked her grandma if she could stay home. Lynda snapped out and said "hell nawl, ain't nothing wrong with you girl". "If I can take my ass to work, you can take that dry ass to school". "Grandma I don't feel good" Cola cried.

"Oh well" Lynda said, "you ain't staying here by yourself, so get yourself together and get the hell out of here and go to school". Cola started getting ready for school. She was only in the fifth grade instead of the sixth grade because Marlene was so busy doing her that she didn't put Cola in school until she was eight years old. The school system put Cola in second grade because she was too old for kindergarten and first grade.

What a morning Cola said to herself as she waited for the bus to go to school. Cola spotted this reddish brown looking Chevy that looked like WaVon's doom buggie.

"I don't believe this shit" Cola spat, "this muther fucker passed me up", Cola yelled "I know you saw me WaVooooooooon". "I'll get his ass" Cola screamed. A few minutes passed by and WaVon passed Cola again, this time with a female in his car.

"OH NO he didn't, this muther crazy…. Little secret my ass wait until this nigga park his shit, he's going to get a rude awakening" Cola said out loud to herself.

WaVon helped his lady friend out the car as Cola looked on, pissed the fuck off. When WaVon entered the building Cola started running saying hold the door please. The young lady that WaVon was with held the door. Cola ran in the hallway out of breath. "Hey Wavon" she tried to sound sexy and sweet. "What's up kid" he said. "Oh now I'm a fucking kid, I wasn't no fucking kid when you was fucking me, was I" Cola said. "Who the fuck is this bitch WaVon" said Cola? "Man", WaVon snapped at Cola "you need to take that shit somewhere else". "Bitch" "who the fuck are you" Wavon's lady friend said?

Cola turned around and before the girl knew it she was on the ground from a sucker punch. "Fuck you mean bitch, fuck all that talking" Cola snapped. "I was trying to be nice. Didn't nobody ask you to put your two cents in and I ain't bout to be lip boxing with your ass" Cola said. Cola and Sabrina (that was the other bitch's name) wrestled for a minute after Sabrina picked herself up off the ground. Once the fight was over they both tried to fix themselves up because they thought they were too cute to be fighting.

WaVon grabbed Cola by the arm and asked her what the fuck she was doing? Cola screamed "how the fuck you gonna pass

Bogus Azz Hood Chick/ PattiCake Taylor 12

me up and the bus stop and not even offer me a ride to school". WaVon laughed and asked her how she been getting to school? "On the damn bus" Cola yelled. "Okay what the fuck is the problem then" WaVon said! "So that's how you gonna act" Cola yelled, "I tell you what you need to do get rid of your friend so we can talk. "WHAT"! WaVon yelled, "take your ass to school and get the fuck out my face".

Cola stood there for a moment thinking of something to say then she said, "I'm feeling a little sick Wavon".

"Maybe I just might go to the doctor to see what's wrong with me" Cola said in anger. "This bitch" he said under his breath. "Sabrina baby" WaVon said, "do me a favor and go home and I'll call you later". "Go HOME"! Sabrina yelled, "oh this bitch telling you what to do now"! "I'll go home but don't worry about calling me no more" Sabrina shouted. "Baby don't act like that" WaVon tried to sound so sweet. "Let me talk to you for a minute" he said. "Hell nawl" Sabrina said, "if you want to talk to me then you need to get rid of that thang over

Bogus Azz Hood Chick/ PattiCake Taylor 13

there in the corner".

WaVon looked back and forth from Cola to Sabrina with begging eyes. Cola stood there with her arms crossed and said "bye Sabrina"! "because I ain't going no where, so what you going to do WaVon" Cola said? "Fuck both of you bitches" he said! WaVon walked away angry as hell at Cola. With everything going on Cola didn't realize what time it was.

Since she was already late for class she decided to go to the basement of the building and hide out until school was over. At 3:30pm Cola came from the basement walked across the street to go in the house acting like she had been in school all day. Little did Cola know the school had already called home.

As soon as Cola walked through the door grandma Lynda B was waiting with a belt in her hand. All you heard was SMACK… smack, smack.

"Ouch" Cola screamed as Lynda smacked Cola again asking her why the school call her at work, when she should've been in school. Crying Cola said the school was lying. "I went to school today grandma "they" through her sobs, they gotta have me confused with someone else". SMACK, "Cola why the hell you lying" Lynda B said in an angry voice. "I'm not grandma you can come up to the school with me tomorrow", Cola said still crying. "Hell that's what I plan on doing" Lynda B said.

Cola had to think of something else to say now because she had just lied to her grandma.

"Graaaaaaaaaaaaandma" Cola said "I can bring a letter from my teacher tomorrow so you don't have to miss work". Lynda B chuckled "that's okay because I'm off tomorrow as for right now you're grounded for two weeks more". "No outside, no telephone calls. "You go to school and bring your narrow ass back home every day on time, do you UNDERSTAND me"? "YEAH" Cola mumble, "SMACK".... "What the hell you mean YEAH". "Yes" grandma Cola said loud and clear. Lynda B sat down at her kitchen table and wondered what the hell was wrong with that child. She tried to give Cola the best. She was tired of Cola stealing and running away. She was tired of Cola being fast. "Eleven year olds don't act like that" grandma Lynda B mumble, "must been them damn drugs Marlene was taking, because I know Alcohol don't make no child act like that". Grandma Lynda B just had to put her foot in Cola ass for stealing her thousand dollars lying as if Marlene had taken it. Lynda B shook her head. I done raised my kids and Marlene gonna have to do the same, time for her to raise her own child.

Cola Krown Blue Royalty Johnson! Lynda B chuckled what the hell was Marlene thinking when she name that child that, "oh she was drunk".

A few months later Cola found herself living back with Marlene since school was out. Marlene only stayed a few blocks up the street from her mother Lynda B. Living with Marlene wasn't a big issue to Cola. Marlene took care of her kids but it was the drinking and getting high that Cola couldn't get with. It always seemed to Cola that Marlene would be a different person, like she had a twin or something. Cola hated

Bogus Azz Hood Chick/ PattiCake Taylor 16

when Marlene drank, she hated being in the same house with her. Not only would Marlene drink and get drunk, she would fight her boyfriends.

Since Marlene couldn't beat up her man she would take it out on Cola. Most of the time Cola would be scared to death, not so much of Marlene but what she might just do to her.

The next day as Cola walked up the street she spotted WaVon's car.

She decided to go up to his crib and knock on the door, knock, knock. "Who is it" WaVon yelled from the other end of the door. "It's Cola, WaVon open the damn door"! "Hell nawl get the fuck away from my door" WaVon yelled. Cola got pissed "aiight nigga I got something for that ass" Cola said to herself. Cola took a brick and busted WaVon's car window.

She was on her second car tire in deep thought when she felt a smack. "What the fuck nigga, I know you didn't just slap the shit out of me". "Oh you gonna pay, mark my words you gonna pay, your ass going to jail". "I wanna see how many nigga's you slap in jail Cola yelled at the top of her lungs". Cola ran home and told Marlene that this dude that stayed across the street from grandma house had raped her. Marlene without thinking rushed her baby girl to the hospital. After five hours of waiting the doctors had examined Cola.

All hell broke loose when the doctors informed Marlene that yes Cola had, had sex but not today. The doctor told Marlene that Cola was no longer virgin.

Marlene blacked out for about five seconds asking the doctor to repeat himself and when he did Marlene went crazy inside the hospital. She started clucking Cola all upside the head with her fist. The doctors couldn't control Marlene they had to call security to help them as Marlene yelled, "just wait until I get your ass home Cola just wait". Marlene put a hurting on Cola until she was tired.

Cola's birthday was soon approaching and she would be twelve years old. Cola wanted to invite everybody to her party including her crush, her next door neighbor Mookie. Cola had

Bogus Azz Hood Chick/ PattiCake Taylor 18

the hot's for him. Mookie was handsome he was fifteen years old. Cola went outside, she saw Mookie cleaning the backyard. Cola was smiling from ear to ear as she watched Mookie clean and show his six pack of abs. Cola stepped closer with a huge grin on her face and boldly asked Mookie was he gonna come to her birthday party. He said yes and then added maybe we will go to Hot Wheels skating rink after. Cola smile got bigger as she said okay maybe.

Marlene decided to give Cola her birthday party only because she was feeling guilty for not being a good parent.

Cola's big day came and Marlene set up for the party. It was summer and Cola knew everything would be cool because Marlene could throw some parties. All the kids in the neighborhood were there, the party was off the chain. Just before the party was over Mookie came and asked Cola to dance.

Cola was acting all geeky as she told him yes. They danced until the party was over and then Mookie popped the big

Bogus Azz Hood Chick/ PattiCake Taylor 19

question. Cola he said, you sure is looking juicy in them purple shorts "will you go with me"? "YES, YES" Cola screamed as if she had won something.

Cola and Mookie had been dating for three months and Cola hadn't give him none yet. Mookie kept pressuring Cola to have sex. Cola had only had sex three times and that's when she spent the night at WaVon's house when she was supposed to been at Gummy's house.

Cola was scared to have sex again after that beat down Marlene had put on her. Marlene told Cola that if she found out she was having sex again she would do everything in her power to break her back bone. Cola been liking Mookie for a long time and she finally got to do the things she dreamed of doing with him like hugging, kissing and telling all the kids Mookie was her boyfriend. Cola was sitting on the porch and Mookie called her over to the fence.

He gave her a kiss and said hey baby. With a smile Cola said hey as her stomach turned into knots. Out of no where Mookie

Bogus Azz Hood Chick/ PattiCake Taylor 20

asked Cola what's it's gonna be? "Because if you not putting out then I need to move on to Tomorrow because she putting out Mookie told her". Tomorrow was a girl who lived up the street, she had two sisters named Today and Yesterday. Tomorrow was real pretty, she was fourteen years old, and was mixed with black and white high yellow as the sun with long curly hair, and all the boys and even some men wanted her. Cola couldn't understand why all the males went crazy over light skinned females as if light was right. "Well I guess it's over Cola said in a low tone". "I thought you were different, I thought you liked me but I guess not huh Mookie"? "You're just like the others boys, you want somebody that's putting out". "What was the big idea" Cola said to herself, "I heard girls saying this or that about sex but I didn't get it, because it wasn't like nothing I had heard". Cola reminisce about how WaVon was humping her for hours and sweating like a pit bull on the street.

School was about to start back in a month, Cola had decided

Bogus Azz Hood Chick/ PattiCake Taylor 21

to put Mookie out her mind and make the best of her summer. Everybody was talking about how Mookie had broken up with Cola for Tomorrow. Cola was heated because she had broken up with Mookie and she refused to be the laughing stock of the summer so she had to make it known.

Cola was looking out the window as she thought of a plan to kick Tomorrow's ass. Cola rushed to put some clothes on because she had a feeling Tomorrow was gonna walk pass to go to Mookie house. Cola beautified herself and then went to sit on the front porch. As Cola sat there listening to a car horn honking, she looked up and lo and behold who was walking down the street, the one and only hot like fire Tomorrow. She was indeed looking good, and Cola wished at that moment she was a man. "Damn" Cola said, "Tomorrow is fine but she won't be after today because I'm gonna cut the bitch face and hell nawl" as if she was talking to somebody else.

"I ain't jealous of that bitch". "I got it going on too to be twelve years old.

Bogus Azz Hood Chick/ PattiCake Taylor 22

I'm pretty as hell, skin like milk chocolate, thick as hell, shaped like a coke bottle". "Tomorrow ain't shit but light skin with long hair and once I give Mookie some of this POP… {pussy of power} he will be back". Cola snapped out of what she was thinking just in time to see Tomorrow.

Cola screamed "hey Tomorrow". Tomorrow turned around with her nose turned up. That's all Cola needed to see, she ran off that porch and grabbed Tomorrow by the hair and started punching her in her head and face. Mookie must have been looking out the window because he came running trying to break up the fight. "Let go of her hair Cola" Mookie yelled, "hell to the nawl" Cola yelled back. A crowd started to form around the fight and Cola really thought she was hard now. As she pulled and pulled on Tomorrow's hair Cola reached in her back pocket and got her scissors, "yelling you think you all that because you light skinned bitch" Cola took them scissors and started swinging to get Mookie away.

Cola then cut a plug of Tomorrow's hair off. Tomorrow

didn't say nothing, just was crying and stuff. Cola was trying her best to use her fist like a bat. Somebody finally broke up the fight Cola turned around asking who broke up a muther fucking fight. "I did BITCH". Cola bald up her fist ready to punch the bitch who broke up her fight but when she turned around it was Marlene standing there with her hand on her hip looking a hot mess with her house coat on and rollers in her hair. "Take your ass in the house now" Marlene yelled. Cola ran in the house as she heard the crowd laughing at her.

Cola knew not to say nothing because Marlene didn't play. Cola didn't want to be no more embarrassed than she had to be. Marlene had put Cola on punishment and Cola was mad because she couldn't go outside.

The next day Marlene left to take care of some business. Cola decided to sneak out the house to go to the park that was across the street from the house. Everybody went there, it wasn't much just a big ass circle where everybody kicked it.

Cola was having a good time dancing to some house music

Bogus Azz Hood Chick/ PattiCake Taylor 24

when Marlene came out of no were and popped Cola upside her head in front of everybody. "Take your ass in the house NOW" Marlene screamed. Cola knew she was in big trouble. Marlene ran up to Cola and beat her across the street. She was clucking Cola where ever she could hit her. Once they made it into the house Marlene started beating Cola with her shoe. Cola tried to run for the door. Marlene tried to snatch Cola as she ran but instead of grabbing Cola, Cola fell into the steel gate that was attached to the door and Cola hit her eye.

   In a matter of seconds her eye looked like someone had hit her with a ton of bricks. Cola jumped up off the floor, ran down to her grandma Lynda's house and started crying all crazy about what Marlene had done to her. Cola begged her grandma to let her come stay with her again and she promise to be good. Marlene was always drinking her favorite drink, (Cola and Crown Blue Royal) and Cola was sick of it. So Cola used her black eye as an excuse to leave Marlene's house.

   Grandma Lynda was mad as hell at what Marlene had done,

so mad that she took Marlene to court to get custody of Cola. Lynda express to the judge that Cola may have been a little bad BUT no child deserved to be abused, not even from the hands of a drunk.

The Judge granted Lynda custody of Cola but Cola was only good for about two weeks. Her eye had healed and it was on like Fred Flintstone.

School was about to start in a few days and Cola was indeed happy that she didn't have to wear her grandma's old fashion sun glasses no more. "Cola" Grandma Lynda yelled "don't you hear me calling you child". "I need you to run to the store". Cola hated going to the store, because her grandma would give her all these colorful dollars that everybody on that thing called welfare would get. When Cola was ready she picked up the colorful food stamps and the note her granny had left.

It was feeling really good outside and Cola was loving it, until she seen that punk muther fucker WaVon.

Cola really hated the sight of him, and never thought much

Bogus Azz Hood Chick/ PattiCake Taylor 26

about him. She was with Mookie at the time but now Cola had no one. As Cola was walking up the street WaVon came running up putting his hands around her waist. Cola was loving it but had to play it off so she didn't seem all thirsty for some attention. "Move your hands nigga" Cola yelled. "Oh you don't love a nigga no more" WaVon said. "Huh" "Cola Krown Blue Royalty Johnson"? "nigga I ain't never love you and I would advised you to leave me the fuck alone before I holla rape". Cola replied.

   WaVon started laughing hard and said just like the last time. "Oh nigga don't laugh to hard because the next time I yell rape you will be going to jail with your ugly ass" Cola said in anger.

   WaVon just laughed again, you know what Cola "you a sorry bitch" and he walked off. Cola yelled in return "your momma the sorry bitch, you fucking child molester fucking a eleven year old".

   Cola finally made it back from the store. As grandma Lynda cooked dinner she yelled to Cola to take her bath so she can eat and go to bed.

Those few days had flown by quick because when Cola woke up the next day it was the first day of school. Cola was excited because she had some new back to school clothes, shoes and book bag. Cola was feeling all jolly until her grandma combed her hair and gave her two ponytails.

"Grandma" Cola said "I don't want two ponytails, can I have one please"? "No" Lynda said, "you only twelve years old, you still a kid". "Since you complaining I'm going to do three ponytails instead, two on the side and one in the back".

Cola hated it. Cola finished getting ready and headed for the bus stop. The bus had arrived and Cola forgot her forty cents on the kitchen table to pay her bus fare. The bus driver threw Cola off the bus just for forty cents. Cola ran in the house to get her bus fare and headed back to the bus stop to wait for another bus. While Cola waited she took her hair down and brushed it into one ponytail. Her hair came down her shoulder and she loved it. The bus was coming, Cola hurried to add carmex to

Bogus Azz Hood Chick/ PattiCake Taylor

her full lips. Cola thought she was fly.

Cola got on the 126 Jackson bus, it stopped right in front of Jackson and Hamlin . As Cola went to sit down she tripped over somebodies feet. Cola looked up and saw Tomorrow. Everybody was laughing at Cola. Cola knew Tomorrow was trying to play hard because she had some people with her. Cola jumped up and reached in her back pocket for a pen so she could stick Tomorrow in the eyes but somebody stopped her and saved Tomorrow's eyeballs.

"Mookie let me go" Cola yelled "this is the second time you saved this high yellow bitch". Her ass is grass and I'm the muther fucking lawn mower". "You've known me my whole life Mookie, and this how you treat me because I won't give you no ass" Cola continue to yelled.

"Cola just stop it", Mookie said, "you always trying to fight somebody, one of these days you gonna get hurt or find yourself in jail, you better think before you react" Mookie said. "Yeah whatever nigga ain't your punk ass on the wrong bus"?

Bogus Azz Hood Chick/ PattiCake Taylor 29

High school the other way or did you drop out" Cola spat?

"Yeah your dusty ass probably dropped out to be with your yellow hoe" Cola yelled loud as ever. Mookie laughed and told Cola she was a salty hater. "I am NOT" Cola screamed and just when her stop came she stole off Mookie and ran off the bus.

Cola sang, it's gonna be a good day because I know somebody got some lunch and school supplies for me, if they don't they gonna get that ass kicked. Just as Cola was finished singing, kids started running up to her as if she was one of the Jackson kids, bringing her all types of stuff.

The week had been great for Cola as she prepared for another day of school. Cola began to wonder why some of the kids were acting weird, some had even stop bringing her stuff to school and others stopped speaking to her. Cola had heard through her G.C {girl click} that she was all mouth and couldn't fight and the only reason she won the fight against Nicole was because Nicole really couldn't fight. Cola couldn't wait until the next day at school because once again she was gonna have to

Bogus Azz Hood Chick/ PattiCake Taylor 30

make an example out of somebody.

It was 2:30pm the bell rang and school was out. Cola ran up to this girl named Heather and asked her what was up. "What do you mean what's up"? Heather asked Cola.

"What the fuck do you mean, what the fuck I mean" Cola yelled at her. "I'm hearing all this shit from my G.C". "What the fuck you or whatever bitch gotta say"?

"Well" Heather yelled back "it's not he say or she say we tired of giving you this and that every year, even your G.C tired of you and somebody needs to stand up to you".

"Now ain't we tired" Heather said loudly with both hands on her hips. Nobody said nothing! "Just what I thought" Cola said with a slight grin on her face. Then out of no where Cola saw some girls and a few boys running her way with sticks and bottles.

One of the girls named Yachi yelled out we gonna get your muther fucking ass. Cola found herself running and running until she passed out and when she woke up she was in the hospital.

The way Cola looked you would have thought the whole school had jumped her. Cola had to miss the rest of the school year. It took her body a while to recover, she was a hot mess.

Summer had once again arrived and Cola was hotter then ever. Some new girls had moved into the building, they were known as the Brown sisters. Sonya was sixteen, Melissa was seventeen and Brandi was eighteen. They all looked different because they all had different daddy's, Melissa looked the best of the three.

Cola found herself hanging with the Brown sisters. She knew she shouldn't because they were too old for her to be hanging with. Cola was only thirteen years old and she was too hot to trot and thought she was grown.

Every morning Cola would get dressed and head down the hallway to kick it. Cola loved hanging around the new girls because their mother was never home. There was always boys, drinks, and weed in there house. Cola began to fall under the

Bogus Azz Hood Chick/ PattiCake Taylor 32

term (birds of A feather flock together).

They had it and Cola wanted it. Nice clothes, shoes, jewelry and they had lots of it. Cola never questioned the Brown sister's on how they got all those things. She just wanted it as well.

Cola soon found out about the lifestyle of the rich and famous, the Brown sister's version. They were thick as thieves and they had Cola in on it. Grandma Lynda was getting really tired of Cola. Cola was stealing from her and Lynda had heard that she was stealing from stores too.

Cola was staying out late and sometimes not even returning home at all. Cola had been doing her own thang and loving it. Grandma Lynda warned Cola that if she didn't get better and mind her she was gonna give her up to D.C.F.S. (department of children and family services).

Cola was like "whatever" to herself knowing that her grandma was just talking shit. "I done heard it all before granny, you ain't gonna do nothing" Cola chuckled letting the words go in one ear out the other.

Bogus Azz Hood Chick/ PattiCake Taylor 33

Melissa walked down the hall to Cola's unit and asked if she could come to their place for a while. Cola told Melissa she would come later once her grandma goes to sleep. Cola thought she was hella cute in her mini skirt and tank top. She headed down the hall for some fun. There was this boy there named Rashard he called himself liking Cola. He was telling Cola sweet nothings. Cola knew they were lies but she fell for them anyways.

Rashard didn't even know Cola like that, so how could he love her. Cola wondered why all boys said they love you when they didn't mean it. Cola knew Rashard just wanted her box cake but it didn't matter to her because she just wanted to have a good time. When Rashard asked how old Cola was, she lied and said sixteen since he was seventeen. Rashard and Cola were in the other room doing the no no good and she was liking it. One thing led up to another and before Cola knew it Rashard was humping on her. Cola didn't think nothing of it, because she couldn't feel nothing so she thought he was

Bogus Azz Hood Chick/ PattiCake Taylor 34

was just grinding on her. When he was done she had all this white stuff on her legs and skirt. "What the hell is this white stuff on me" Cola screamed . "It's nut bitch" said Rashard! "What the fuck did you say to me"? Cola yelled. "I said it's NUT B"…. before Rashard could get the bitch word out Cola was throwing a beer bottle at his head. Rashard and Cola was yelling at each other and once again Cola yelled rape.

"Bitch I didn't rape you, you gave it to me hoe" Rashard yelled. "I didn't give you shit because I didn't feel shit" Cola yelled back at him. "But I tell you what, you can say goodbye to your freedom because I'm calling the muther fucking Po-Po and I'm telling them that you raped a minor". "I'm only thirteen years old, I got all your white stuff on me and you going to jail" Cola yelled. "Bitch" he yelled, "get your lying, ugly ass up out of here".

"Rashard, you little dick muther fucker, I ain't gonna be to many more bitches" Cola yelled. "Sonya how old is this B"…? Cluck Cola went upside Rashard head with a beer bottle.

Bogus Azz Hood Chick/ PattiCake Taylor 35

Rashard was coming for Cola but his boys stopped him. Cola ran out the house after she dialed 911 and left the phone off the hook.

Cola went into the house and was in tears as she saw her bags packed. "Grandma why is my suitcase at the door" Cola said through her tears. Grandma Lynda told Cola because she was tired of her bullshit and that they were going to court in the morning because she didn't want custody anymore. Cola dried her eyes all while knowing her grandma was just lying like all the other times.

A month later and two rescheduled court dates Cola, Marlene and Grandma Lynda were finally in front of the judge. Lynda had explained the situation to the judge which he already knew because he was the same court judge that gave Lynda custody of Cola after Cola fell into the steel frame of Marlene's gates and messed her eye up. Marlene begged the judge, she was trying to step up to the plate but it was too late. Marlene cried her heart out.

Bogus Azz Hood Chick/ PattiCake Taylor 36

She cried to the judge about how she wanted her daughter back, that she promised she would be a good parent. The judge had Marlene's old file and it didn't sit well with him. He told Marlene she would have to get herself together, get a larger place to live in and go to an eight week A.A meeting in order to get Cola back. The judge then turned back to Lynda and asked her if she was sure she wanted to turn Cola over to the system.

Lynda looked at Cola as tears ran down her face and then turned back to the judge and said yes you honor, I'm sure.

It was all over from that point Cola started screaming, falling to the floor and kicking as the guards tried to take her to the back.

Cola even tried to reach for one of the guards gun but couldn't get it loose. Cola was yelling at the top of her lungs I hate you! "I hate you grandma and I will never forgive you".

A caseworker placed Cola in a room for most of the day. A few hours later she finally came to get Cola and informed her that they had founded a temporary home for her to go to until a permanent home became available.

Cola was placed in her first foster home. Dorothy Wilson was her foster mothers name. She already had some girls living in her house. Cola was scared out here mind living with people she didn't even know.

Cola was placed on the south side of Chicago a part of town she had never been to before given that she had been raised on the west side. The south side and west side were two different sides of Chicago.

Amelia one of Cola's foster sisters asked her to come outside and play but Cola wanted to stay in and play house, this was something that Sonya would play with Cola when no one else was around. "How do you play that" Amelia asked? "Well one of us be the momma and the other one be the daddy" said Cola. Cola didn't know that Ms. Wilson had been listening to their conversation.

"COLA" Ms. Wilson yelled, "I'm not raising no dykes up in here so you need to chill with that shit right here and right now,

Bogus Azz Hood Chick/ PattiCake Taylor 38

DO YOU UNDERSTAND"!

   Ms. Wilson kept Cola away from the other girls and moved her room to the basement of the house. She informed Cola not to leave her room unless she was told. Cola was sitting on her bed confused, "DYKE" what the hell is that? Cola was happy when her caseworker Mr. Smith told her she would be moving in a couple of days. Cola was happy as hell to be leaving out of Ms. Wilson's house, the night before Cola was gonna leave she added bleach to Ms. Wilson shampoo.

   The next day Cola went to her new foster home. Her foster mothers name was Rose Jackson and she had two biological daughters named April and May. April was seventeen and May was twelve. They both were high yellow and Cola couldn't stand them already.

   Ever since Mookie started dating Tomorrow all love for light skinned chicks went out the window. To Cola's surprise everything with the sisters was going well until Halloween came around. They were gonna have a Halloween party and this

Bogus Azz Hood Chick/ PattiCake Taylor 39

was the worst day of Cola's life.

The day she would never forget because April and May made her feel some type of way. April was gonna be a Queen and May was gonna be a Princess but when it came time for Cola to decide what she was gonna be. April told her she should be Cicely from the color purple.

Cola was so hurt that she started to get angry. "Why would they pick someone who america think's is one of the ugliest women in the world".

After that the names just kept coming, tar baby, monkey, oreo black stuff. It got so bad that they even made a song out of oreo black stuff. They would sing "oreo black stuff, who do you think you are, you so black but you want to be light". Cola couldn't take it no more, no one ever called her names like this before.

Cola tried to slice her wrists with a blade. Cola was passed out in the bathroom when April came banging on the door for her to come out. When Cola never did April busted the

Bogus Azz Hood Chick/ PattiCake Taylor 40

bathroom door open and founded Cola on the floor. April yelled calling her mom.

Rose came running to the bathroom and saw Cola passed out, she told April to call 911. After being discharged from the emergency room, they all made it back home and Rose demanded to know what was going on before she called Mr. Smith.

Cola told her foster mom that she wasn't happy being in her home, that her kids picked on her and called her name's. Rose became very angry with her children. "You know I didn't raised you two like that" Rose said to the girls, "so tell me what's the problem is"? April and May explained how they were a little jealous of Cola because she was getting more attention.

The next day Cola's caseworker Mr. Smith came by to talked to Rose. After doing so he spoke with Cola alone, telling her that black is beautiful, and that no matter what her skin tone is she should always cherish who she is.

Cola's attitude seem to change, Cola was a pretty girl but

now she thought she was the finest thirteen year old on the south side of Chi city.

Cola had been getting a lot of attention from the neighborhood boys and it had gone to her head. Cola had become very wild and active, sleeping with any boy that told her she was cute. She wanted attention and Cola didn't care where it came from. Cola began to stay out late and that's when she met TyYuan, he was twenty years old. Cola had lied and told him she was seventeen.

For most of their relationship TyYuan was good to Cola, that was until the boys in the hood started talking about how Cola gave good head. TyYuan was pissed because Cola wasn't giving him head.

When TyYuan approached Cola with what was going on she tried to tell him that those boys was lying and that they were just hating because he had a cutie with a booty. "What the hell is head" asked Cola? "I don't give head". TyYuan didn't believe her, he beat her up real bad. Cola was in pain, crying, and she couldn't believe TyYuan was a woman beater. He locked her in his house until her black eyes and swollen lip went down.

When Cola finally went home Rose, Mr. Smith and the police were at the house. They had been looking for Cola for over two weeks. Rose had already packed Cola's things, she was informed that Cola would be moved from her home. Cola was transferred to another home in the 100's, wild 100's is what she heard it was called.

Cola had been placed in three foster homes in six months. Cola was now beginning to miss her family. Her fourteenth birthday was coming up and she was hoping that Marlene wouldn't let her down.

Cola made plans to run away to her mom's crib, she didn't want to spend her birthday with what's her face (the new foster parent) and her family. Cola was sick of all these old nagging foster mothers, who really didn't care, and just wanted a pay check.

Bogus Azz Hood Chick/ PattiCake Taylor 43

The weekend had come and Cola tried her best to settle into her new home. Cola felt a little uneasy with this foster mother, something wasn't right about Margaret Douglas.

Cola made a mental note to leave once Margaret went to bed and way before she woke up the next morning. Cola took a bath and put on her smell good so when the time came all she had to do was freshen up, brush her teeth and be up.

It was six am and Cola was getting ready. She combed her hair, put on her pretty sundress, and her cute wedge heel sandals.

Cola was all ready to hit the road, she grabbed her oversize purse, "leave everything else behind and hit the door" she said to herself. There was only one problem, as Cola locked herself out the house she realized that she didn't know how to get back to the west side.

Cola decided she would just hitch a ride because she didn't know how to catch the bus from where she was. As she strolled the street, horns were honking something serious. Cola

Bogus Azz Hood Chick/ PattiCake Taylor 44

wondered if they thought she was a prostitute or something. After a few guys rode passed, there was one guy that caught her attention. He was fine as hell, light skinned with a Jeri Curl and when he pulled over Cola noticed he had hazel eyes.

Cola may not have liked light skinned girls but a man was a different story. He was a must have Cola thought to herself. "Hey sexy Chocolate" he said to her, what's your name? Cola smiled and said Chocolate and yours? "Terrance but call me Terry" he said, "do you need a ride"? "How did you know" she giggled? "Because you've been running through my mind all day and your feet look tired" Terry replied back.

Cola just laughed and said "nigga please you don't even know me". "Well I want to get to know ya lil mama " Terry said with a smile. "Well you can get to know me while you drive me out west" Cola replied back. "Aiiight" he said, "but can I spend some time with you first then take you out west"? "That's cool, I just need to be out west before dark" Cola said with a smile wider then the smile Terry had. Cola got into

Bogus Azz Hood Chick/ PattiCake Taylor 45

Terry's car, as they rode, he asked her a million and one questions.

"How old are you sexy chocolate" Terry asked? "I'm eighteen, and how old are you hulk of handsome" Cola replied? "I'm thirty I guess I'm too old for you huh" Terry replied!

"Hell to the yeah but it's cool" Cola said. "So what we gonna do"? She asked. "Let's go to my crib Terry said and then I'll take you to dinner". Cola was excited, nobody had ever taken her out to dinner before. She was hoping he wasn't talking about Burger King either.

They arrived at Terry's house, he lived in his momma's basement. He had it fixed up very nicely, Cola thought that was odd for a man. As Cola relaxed on the futon Terry fixed them some gin and juice. Cola gobbled hers down and asked for another one before Terry could sit down good. Terry was happy to fix Cola another drink, she didn't notice him dropping something in her drink.

Terry turned on some slow groove music and Cola jumped

up dancing all over the place as if he was playing house music or something. Cola finally passed out and Terry had his way with her for hours. When he was done with her he drove her to the Dan Ryan expressway with a sheet over her body and left her there.

Cola finally came too jumping up and screaming like she was nuts asking for help. She didn't remember anything except that last drink. Finally someone came over to save her, Cola was scared to death. She didn't know what happen or where she was at. Some young woman ran over to Cola asking her what happened.

Cola told the young woman that she didn't remember a thing. The young lady asked Cola her name. "Cherri" Cola replied and yours? Peaches she said, "Do you need to go to the hospital"? "No I'm fine, I just need to get home, can you take me home" Cola asked. "No problem girl, I just need to pick up my roommate Cream first because we're running late for work".

Cola said "okay that's cool I just need to get to the west

side ASAP". Peaches went into the trunk of her car and got some clothes out, here girl she said looks like we the same size. Cola was grateful for the clothes because all she had to her name at that moment was a sheet. Cola and Peaches rode to the east side, this area was pretty nice it was called Hype Park.

Cola was trying to make conversation so she asked Peaches what she did for a living. "Cream and I are dancers, strippers, hoes or whatever you want to call it, you know people look down on our job". "A stripper"? Cola asked as she laughed.

"Hell yeah girl", Peaches got excited, "nigga's be flocking with them dollars". "For real"? "shiiiiit I need some of those dollars because my birthday coming up and I'm flat broke" Cola said. "When is your birthday"? Peaches asked.

"July 7" Cola said nice and proudly. Mines to Peaches screamed! "CANCER" they both said together. So Cherri how old are ya? "I'm eighteen going on nineteen" Cola said, "but everybody seem to think I'm thirteen, telling me I look young but got a grown ass woman body". "Cherri giiiiirl I can make you look your age" Peaches said with a smile, "just wait until we get to the crib". Peaches and Cream had a huge two bedroom apartment on 67th and Woodlawn. Hey Cream, Peaches said "this is Cherri and it's a long story how we met so I'll tell you later".

"In the mean time we need to hook this girl up like a DIVA" "Bam"! Peaches was getting herself together while Cream was giving Cherri the hook up. Peaches gave Cola a nice fitted outfit with some five inch stiletto heels, Cola almost fell as she tried to walk in them. Cream did Cola's hair and added a little makeup to enhance her features. Cola thought she was hot to deaf, she was loving her new look.

After all three of them were done, they look like high class strippers. Looking at Peaches and Cream, you would have never known that they shook a tail feather for cash. They headed out the door and got into Cream's Benz to head to the hottest club on 71st and Halsted, it was called the Pole in the wall. Every man and some women for that matter knew if you

Bogus Azz Hood Chick/ PattiCake Taylor 49

wanted some P.A.T {pussy, ass, & tits} the Pole in the wall was the place to be.

They arrived at the club looking flawless. All eyes were on them as they walked to the front of the club. Cola being smart at the mouth busted out and said "It must be a reason for eyeball season" because all eyes on US! Nobody said nothing because Peaches and Cream had them baller thugs who would shoot a nigga without thinking. Nobody fuck with Gee, Pee, and

Dee's girls, they knew better.

Peaches introduced Cherri to the fella's. It was show time and Peaches had to go and get ready so she asked Dee to look after Cola until she was done. Dee was trying to holla at Cola but she wasn't going, she was trying to play hard to get. Dee offer to buy her a drink. "No thanks" Cola said remembering what had just happened hours ago. "I don't drink anymore but that's nice of you Dee". Cola made a mental note, if she ever saw that punk nigga Terry again he would pay.

Bogus Azz Hood Chick/ PattiCake Taylor 50

As Dee and Cola talked some girl name "Jazzy Q be Me" was on stage performing. "Baby girl had a nice body but that face was a hot mess dot com who the hell let her out the cage". Cola laughed to herself and thought her name should have been pizza face Jazzy Q with all them lumps and bumps on her face.

Cola got excited when she heard Peaches and Cream was coming to the stage to do an girls act. This was not Cola first time having these type of feelings for girls. After playing house with Sonya, Cola kinda liked it!

When the club ended, the girls were getting ready to head out when Dee asked Cola for her number. "Ummmm" Cola said "I can't give out my number". "Why not" he said? "Because I don't have a home phone" Cola replied. Dee got pissed and told Cola to stop lying.

"If you don't want me to have your number just say so" Dee yelled. "I'm not lying" Cola said with a slight attitude, "I ain't gotta lie to you, I don't have a home phone". Cola was embarrassed to tell anyone she was a ward of the state. "Here"

Bogus Azz Hood Chick/ PattiCake Taylor 51

Dee said, "Take my pager and when you see 773-123-4567, call back and don't take all fucking day, if you see 911 behind it stop what your ass is doing and hit my line". Cola was looking cross eyed at him, "who the fuck did he think he was talking to".

Cola just laughed it off and said okay! The guys kissed the girls as they said their good-byes. The boys had to go and handle some major business so they wouldn't be caking it with the ladies until another day.

Peaches asked Cola if she wanted to stay at their place or go out west. Cola said she would stay with them, since she had enjoyed the earlier part of the night with them.

Cola hadn't thought about her new foster mother or her new foster home all day. Cola was sitting at the kitchen table eating like a starved child. "Damn" Cola said "this pizza good as hell". Cola began to look sad, not knowing what was gonna happen to her once her case worker got a hold of her. "Damn" Cola said a little too loud. "What's wrong" Cream asked with concern on her face. "I just want to move out my mom house so bad, but I can't afford it" Cola said in a low tone.

Peaches and Cream look at each at the same time and said you can move in with us. I'll get you a job at The Pole in the Wall if you want Peaches said!

"Hell to the yeah" Cola said, I see all them twenty's you got, "bout how much you make tonight"? "It's only eight hundred dollars, it was a slow night" Peaches said as if it was nothing. Cherri's eyes got big, "eight hundred dollars"? "Girl fly, that's a lot in my book" Cola replied in an over excited tone.

The next morning they were in the living room eating breakfast and watching T.V. Cream so happen to turn to the news just in time to hear there cover story.

Breaking News we are looking for a missing thirteen year old African American girl by the name of Cola Krown Blue Royalty Johnson. She's 5'3 130lbs, dark complexion with shoulder length hair. We will have a photo within the hour. If

Bogus Azz Hood Chick/ PattiCake Taylor 53

anyone has any information on Cola Krown Blue Royalty Johnson, please call your local Police department.

Cola damn near choked on her food. Cream ran to pat Cola on the back "what's wrong" Cream asked. Cola told her that, the girl on the news was her sister and she needed to get to the west side fast. Cola was scared out her mind.

After lying to Peaches and Cream she knew it was a matter of time before they found out the news report was about her.

"Bitch ass" Ms. Douglas done called the Po-Po on me Cola said with anger.

As Peaches drove up Independence blvd Cola asked her to let her out on Jackson and Hamlin. Cola thanked Peaches for everything and got out of the car and walked the two blocks to her mom's house. As soon as Cola walk through her momma's door the police came out of no where.

Marlene was screaming and hollering like a mad woman. Marlene was so happy to see Cola that she greeted her with a cluck upside the head for having everybody worry about her.

Bogus Azz Hood Chick/ PattiCake Taylor 54

Mr. Smith Cola's caseworker got out his car. He informed the police and all that was involved in the situation that this was a D.C.F.S matter and it will be taken care of. Mr. Smith hauled Cola off to another foster home.

The agency decided to try something different and place Cola far out so they took her out to Lynwood Illinois. Cola's new foster mom was a lady named Pearl Rice, "Damnnnnnnnn", Cola said under her breath this woman must got money.

Her crib was off the chain, sharp as hell. She had a Cadillac and a Lexus in her garage. She even had a pool in her backyard.

Cola was shocked because you didn't see no pool in no backyards in the hood. "Cola", COLA Mr. Smith said, "what you day dreaming about"? "Shit" Cola said. "Young lady watch your damn mouth" Mr. Smith replied.

Cola laughed out loud and walked away. Mr. Smith explained to Ms. Rice that Cola was a high risk foster kid, she was a runaway, and a thief, he told Ms. Rice to be careful. Since Ms. Rice had a nice home the state thought it would be a good idea to try and move Cola far to keep her from the city and show her that she can have nice things if she stays out of trouble. Cola was unpacking when she chuckled to herself. "I ain't no dummy these burbs ain't gonna hold me down".

Just as she was in mid thought, she heard a beeping noise. It was that pager Dee had given her. Ten missed pages, "gat damn" Cola said "and you ain't even got the draws yet".

"What's up" Cola said into the phone. "What's up" said the female caller. "What the fuck you doing with my man's pager" the female said?

"Baby girl" Cola said! "If he was your man then he wasn't last night, he was all in this box cake, calling my name... "Cherrrrrrrri, Pa Pow BOOM Kack KACK dot BAM"!!! "He was spending all his money on me, so now "BITCH" what that do" Cola said and hung up in the female face. Ring, ring, ring, Cola stood there looking at the phone, seeing that same number she just called from Ms. Rice's phone, Cola decided she better answer. Cola yelled in the phone, "yeah hoe you don't want this so state the issue and state it quick". "Bitch" the female said, "let me speak to Ty". "Who"? Cola spat. "Tyrone bitch did I stutter" said the female caller. "Ain't no Tyrone here, I don't even know no Tyrone you dumb bitch".

"CLICK"! Cola hung up again. Ring, ring, ring.... "Bitch didn't I tell you ain't noTyrone here". "Hold on shorty!!, slow your muther fucking role, this Darnell"! "Darnell who"? Cola yelled. "Dee the person pager you got". "Oh" Cola said "what's up with you baby"? "You" Dee said, "I want to know what's up with you. I thought about you all night". "Yeah right" Cola thought, "who in the hell was that female that just paged your goofy ass" Cola mumble. "What you say shorty"? Dee said. "Nothing" said Cola

  "So you've been thinking about me but you just now paging the pager"? "Well some bitch paged it, I guess boy" said Cola "Don't I guess me, baby" Dee said. "Dee I ain't slow, who was that bitch" Cola said in a pitch tone. Dee ignored Cola.

  "I know you need a good man in your life to hold your fine

ass down" Dee said trying to change the subject. "No not really" Cola laughed "phony ass nigga". "I don't need no man in my life". "But if you really trying to be my man I need you to come get me cause I'm hungry".

Dee said "cool baby I'm on my way what's the address"? Cola told him and they hung up. As Cola was getting herself together Ms. Rice walked in on her and asked her what she was doing? Cola looked Ms. Rice up and down and then said with a smart mouth "I'm going outside for a little while". "Oh no you not Ms. Lady, did you asked me if you can go out"?

Your caseworker already informed me that you are a runaway. You're only thirteen years old, you don't run nothing around here" Ms. Rice said

"EXCUSE you"! "I'm fourteen, my birthday is today but of course you wouldn't know that because you didn't read my file. All you seen is dollars signs". "I bet I go outside", Cola mumbled under her breath. "You leave up out of here and see what happens" Ms. Rice tried to put some fear in Cola. I swear

Bogus Azz Hood Chick/ PattiCake Taylor 58

Ms. Rice said, "you give a child a foot and they try and jump a mile"!

A couple of hours had passed and Cola hadn't heard from Dee Cola called the number she talked to Dee from but she didn't get an answer. Cola waited another thirty minutes before calling the burn out cellphone he had, this time she got an answer.

"Hello" the male voice answered, "Yeah can I speak to Dee" Cola said! "I'm sorry Darnell is a little tied up". "May I ask who's calling" the male voice asked?

"Who the fuck wants to know" Cola yelled. "Young lady" he said, "you need to watch your language and answer the question I'm about to ask you, what's your relation to Darnell"? "I'm his girlfriend and I want to know what's taking him so long to come and get me". "What's your name" the man asked? "Cherri" Cola said, "damn what's up with all these damn questions"?

"Cherri" he said, "is that your government name"? "No

Bogus Azz Hood Chick/ PattiCake Taylor 59

WHY"! Cola asked? "I just asked you what's up with these damn questions" said Cola. Click the male caller hung up. Ring, ring ring, "Hello" the male caller said. "Why the fuck" Cola began. "Young lady" the man screamed, "watch your mouth and listen real carefully". "There's been an accident and I need you to contact Darnell's parents right now". "Hold up wait a minute, I just met this nigga the other day". Cola heard another click in her face before she could finish her statement. "This is some crazy shit" Cola said to herself.

    Pearl called Cola down for dinner. Cola ate, took her a nice bath and laid in her king size bed. A huge step from the couch and twin bed that she was use too. Cola got comfortable, turned on her 32inch tube television and started watching her favorite program. GLOW "Gorgeous Ladies of Wrestling". After that she flicked the channel but nothing was on. Cola turned to channel 7 news and hit the lights to go to sleep until she heard the reporter say three black males shot to death on Chicago Ave and Homan.

Bogus Azz Hood Chick/ PattiCake Taylor 60

"Shit" Cola jumped up out the bed, "that's the west side". Cola almost hit the floor, her eyes was glued to the T.V. "All shit" she spat "that's Peaches and Cream jumping up and down and screaming like they crazy". "Hold the fuck up", Cola mind started racing, "that car looks so familiar, oh hell nawl that's WaVon's shit".

Cola was stuck in thought, wondering why WaVon's car was there and why Peaches and Cream were there, it didn't make sense. Cola needed a way to get out west so that she could be nosy. "Damn I need a plan, how the fuck am I gonna get out west" Cola mind wandered. "Oh yeah" she said to herself "just wait till that heifer goes to sleep and I'm going to steal one of her cars and find my way out west". "Damn" Cola laughed out loud, "I don't even know how to drive". "But hell, I done seen enough people drive". "That shit should be easy".

Pearl finally went to sleep after she thought Cola was asleep. Cola creep to the garage and got into Pearl's Cadillac. She turned it on, put the car in drive and tried to ease out but Cola hit the gas a little too hard and the car went flying through Pearl's living room. Pearl ran down the stairs to see what happened. Her eyes got big as day as she pull Cola from the driver side and started clucking her upside the head. Cola had a flash back of Marlene hitting her, just then she threw Pearl to the floor and starting stomping her.

Cola found herself in a juvenile detention center for two years. She had stomped that poor woman into a coma. Once Cola was released she was shipped off to another foster home. As she rode in peace she thought about something she hadn't thought about in a long time, Dee, Peaches and the crew she even thought about WaVon. Cola never did found out what happened that night.

Cola felt she was just too young for all the bull shit she was going through. She was now sixteen and headed up the wrong path. Mr. Williams, Cola's new caseworker pulled up to a house on 71st and Morgan.

"Cola your new foster mother's name is Ms. Marilyn Miller

Bogus Azz Hood Chick/ PattiCake Taylor 62

and if you want the system to let you go home to your family you need to try and obey this foster mother". "At your age you've been in too many foster homes and that just don't look good". "If you're not careful you will be heading to a group home". "Come on" Mr. Williams said, "let's go meet your new foster mother". When Mr. Williams left Cola met Ms. Miller son too!

He was fiiiiiiine! He had to be at least twenty five years old and I, "Cola Krown Blue Royalty Johnson", had to have him. Cola wasn't a little girl no more, since she had started having sex.

Her body had filled out more than ever and her case manger at the juvenile center let her know it too. He was fat and ugly, had to be forty five or so. He was making Cola have sex with him every night. Most of the time he was juicing her legs because his penis was small and he had a triple stomach. He wasn't the first case Manger to have sex with Cola. "Hell" Cola said "I might as well do it for enjoyment".

Bogus Azz Hood Chick/ PattiCake Taylor

Ms. Miller told Cola to head to bed so she could get up early to enroll in school. Cola did as she was told.

The months had flew by. Cola liked high school for the most part but had a very hard time staying focused. All the boys wanted some of her (fresh meat) is what they called her. Cola had began to find love in boys and even some men sleeping around like some whore.

People on the outside looking in, might have thought Cola was a fool but she wasn't she got paid to get laid and her pockets were fat! She used her looks and that coke a cola body to get what she wanted. Cola dated a few guys in school. She wasn't worried about getting caught up either because there was a known rule at school if you didn't belong to the gang on that floor you got your ass beat if you was caught where you didn't belong.

Cola made sure to date one boy from each gang. It was crazy how if you lived on one side of the street you belonged to this gang and if you lived on the other side you belonged to that

Bogus Azz Hood Chick/ PattiCake Taylor

gang but you all had to go to the same school in the hood. Cola went to school every day starving for attention. She was lonely and depressed and founded happiness in fucking.

There was this clique of girls in school called Colors, everybody in the clique had the name of a color. There were five girls so far Red, Black, White, Yellow and Brown. It was kinda funny why they had those Colors as names.

Red and Yellow were light skinned, Black was black as tar, Brown was brown skin and White was damn near just that, white. Cola wanted to be a part of the Colors. Cola walked up to Red and said, "what's the biz I'm Purple, that's my favorite color and I want to be in this clique".

Red did a double take to her girls and then looked at Cola and said "bitch who you talking too"?

Cola did a double take and then slapped the shit out of Red. Red looked up and told Cola she had a lot of heart for hitting her. Right then Cola knew the Colors Clique was soft because if they weren't that whole crew would have beat her ass.

Bogus Azz Hood Chick/ PattiCake Taylor 65

Cola walked away as Red and her crew watched her. Red told her girls that Cola had heart but if she EVER… before Red could finish what she was saying she received a flying lock in her eye. Cola walked back up to the crew with a smile and said "bitch you got a little too much lip for me, you ain't shit but mouth". "I proved my point not once but twice SO as of NOW I'm the head pussy in charge".

"I'm muther fucking Purple, now have y'all ass outside at 3:00pm so we can have a meeting and by the way, Red take your swollen eye ass to the school nurse". This time when Cola walked away nobody said nothing.

Cola and the Color crew met up after school then headed to the park to discuss what they were going to do over the weekend.

They decided to go skating, every Saturday The Colors were at Route 999. Route 999 was nothing like Hot Wheels skating rink but it would do.

The Colors crew even wore colors that match their names,

Bogus Azz Hood Chick/ PattiCake Taylor 66

they thought they were hot as pancakes. The crew really didn't skate, they went to dance and get all the attention from the boys and ugly looks from the girls. There was this one boy who was checking Cola out after seeing her one too many times. He decided to approach her with his mack game. "What's the deal baby girl" he said to her, "Your looking so fine you blowing my mind". Cola turned around and said "you looking so fine I want to fuck you right now".

"Damn baby girl you get right to the point don't you" he said. "Ain't that what you want" Cola asked, "you wanna fuck right".

Old boy just looked at Cola for a moment and said "NO, but I would like to make love to you when you become my lady".

Cola just laughed, and then looked at him for a minute, "what's your name" she asked, "Daddy B" he said, and "you're Purple, you sixteen and now I'm your man". "Whatever" Cola said laughing and "how old are you"? "Nineteen" replied Daddy B.

Bogus Azz Hood Chick/ PattiCake Taylor 67

"Nineteen, nigga please tell me what you can do with a sixteen year old because you can't control me". "I'm a young lady and you will have to treat me that way". Cola spat.

It was closing time at the skating rink, Daddy B asked Cola for her number and if he could take her home. Daddy B took Cola home alright, right to his place. Daddy B rolled up a joint and fixed them some drinks, he went to the bathroom after turning his boom box on. While he was gone Cola switched drinks, thinking about what happen last time a man fixed her a drink. She reminisced about how she saw Terry again at the gas station, that muther fucker should never do shit to nobody with that big ass birth mark on his face. While Terry was inside the gas station, Cola took the gas off the pump and pumped the gas in the back seat of his car. Terry didn't notice because he was too busy arguing with the clerk about how he gave her twenty, and not ten dollars on pump five.

He was so pissed that he didn't pump his gas or even realize the smell of gas in his car. He started his car, lit his cigarette and the car burst into flames. All Cola could do was stand there and chuckle to herself. "Now you a dumb fuck, I bet you won't throw nobody else on the Dan Ryan expressway".

Daddy B came back from the bathroom and downed his drink. Cola waited five minutes and nothing happened. When Daddy B noticed Cola was in space some where he reached over and downed her drink too. "Daaaaaaaaaaamn" Cola said to herself he downed his drink and mines too and wasn't nothing even wrong with it.

Daddy B leaned over to kiss Cola. He put his tongue all up in her mouth as they exchanged sweet juices of the tongue french kissing. Daddy B leaned on Cola a little more and she fell back on the couch. Daddy B kissed her face, her ear and those so soft sweet full lips. He turned her over to rubbed her back. He rub her back so gently. He began to play in Cola's hair and when he realized it wasn't weave he pulled it and kissed Cola on her neck. Daddy B caressed her tits through her shirt, he was getting a little excited as he removed her shirt.

Bogus Azz Hood Chick/ PattiCake Taylor 69

Daddy B started to take off his clothes. While he was taking off his clothes Cola told him to give her a second.

"I'll be right back" she said with a smile. Cola picked up her purse and went into the bathroom. She pulled out her towel, soap and body spray. After Cola freshened up she came out the bathroom ass hole naked. Daddy B did a double take, "damn girl", he said, bring that ass over here. Daddy B didn't waste no time, he must have known that Cola washed her box cake because he went straight for her pussy.

Daddy B, licked and sucked Cola pearl tongue so softly. Cola lost all control, "wh…what you doing to me, ain't nobody ever did this to me before". Daddy B was the first to give Cola oral sex. She started to shake and scream while doing so she called out his name and telling him how good it felt. As Cola told him she was cumin again she choked on her saliva. After it was all over, Cola fell into a deep sleep.

The next day Daddy B took Cola out for breakfast then dropped her off in front of her house. Daddy B gave her a kiss and told her he would call her later. Cola was feeling her some Daddy B, that's it, that's all! Everything else would have to come to an end!

"Fuck the colors" Cola said out loud, "all I want is some BIG DADDY B" laughing to herself she said "Big Daddy Dick that is"!

As Cola headed in the house, Marilyn (Cola's foster mother) had her hand on her hip. "Ms. Thang" she said, "where have your fast tail been"?

Cola lowered her head and said, "I was at my friend Walkeisha's house". "They telephone was cut off and I couldn't call, I'm sorry" she said. Marilyn put Cola on telephone punishment since her friend didn't have one so she said. Cola begged her foster mother to put her on outside punishment instead but Marilyn didn't give in.

Cola loved the telephone and every time it rang it was for her. "Cola", Marilyn called "go to Walgreens and pick up my medication". Cola was happy to go, so she could steal her a phone. She refused to not be able to talk to her Daddy B. Marilyn was a big plus size woman, she would never make it to the phone in time. "I know she wouldn't even be smart enough to think I got an extra phone" Cola said laughing to herself.

After about a week or so Cola decided to give Daddy B the run down on Marilyn she knew that would make him buy her a brand new brick cell phone. Daddy B had a little drug spot on the low end. Everyday Cola would leave school early to go and sit on the block with him.

Daddy B had been doing things for Cola that no other man had ever done before and Cola was falling for him hard.

A few months had passed and Cola stopped hanging out with the Colors, they had become very violent when she wasn't around. There was this girl named Banessa, Ban Ban is what everybody called her. She was beyond pretty and Black was envious of her because her so called man was trying to cake it with Ban Ban. Black had gotten knocked up and after she had her baby her so called man told her he wasn't into chubby girls.

Bogus Azz Hood Chick/ PattiCake Taylor 72

"I ain't no chubby chaser" he said. "Ban Ban is 36-22-36 yup yup! I gotta have that". "She's hot and sorry Black you NOT"!!

Black was pissed and she was gonna make Ban Ban pay for it. Black made up some story so the Colors could help her jump Banessa. Banessa was walking from computer class when Black came out of no where and knocked her to the floor. Red passed Black a blade and she cut Banessa's face. Ban Ban looked like Freddy from Nightmare On Elm Street had attack her when Black was done.

Cola stood there in shock, she couldn't believe her eyes. The school security tried to break it up but it was too late, Black had done a job on Banessa. Cola started to vomit at the site of the blood. Cola's stomach started hurting, she went to the school nurse and the nurse told her she was pregnant and she needed to be checked out by a doctor.

Cola went to the doctor and founded out that she was three months pregnant. She cried at first but then she thought, Daddy B would be a good Daddy!

Bogus Azz Hood Chick/ PattiCake Taylor 73

Word traveled fast, the Police wasted no time arresting Black. After a few months of sitting behind bars Future Success Hale, better known as Black had to serve fifteen years to life for the murder of Banessa Mona Reese who died after losing so much blood. The judge was not playing with that ass.

Cola had taken a week off from school, she told her foster mother she was sick. Marilyn told Cola that she couldn't miss any more days of school. Cola wasn't trying to hear what Marilyn was talking about.

Cola turned around to leave and Marilyn took her frozen chicken out the sink and threw it at Cola.

Cola in return threw the chicken back at her foster mom, that left a knot upside Marilyn's head.

Cola just wanted to be under her Daddy B. She was so excited about the baby that she broke her neck damn near to go tell him. She didn't want to tell him on the phone, she wanted to see the shock on his face! Cola made it to the spot were Daddy B held down his own shit, he didn't trust nobody with his money. He had to make a example out of Stepfon when his money was short last week.

After seeing Stepfon with an broken arm and leg nobody wanted it from Daddy B. Cola ran up to Daddy B, "baby guess what" she said, "I'm three months pregnant". Daddy B acted so excited, but in the back of his mind he knew he wasn't the daddy, He had been fucking Cola for two months, but he went along with the program anyways because he was kinda digging shorty.

After Cola returned to school she was asked to transfer to an all girl pregnant school, "it would be in the best interest of the baby" the school nurse told her.

Cola woke up one morning not feeling her best. She went to the clinic and the doctor told her that she had an abnormal pap smear and to come back in a few days for the results. When Cola got up to walk she felt a sharp pain in her side. It went away for a brief second and then it hit real hard. Cola passes out and when she woke up she was in the hospital and no longer pregnant. Although Cola was sad that she had lost her baby she figured that everything happens for a reason good or bad. She was too young to have a baby anyway.

Cola stayed at home for two weeks before going back to school but the day that she returned turned out to be her last day. School didn't interest her no more, all she wanted was to be around her big dick Daddy B and his money. Cola talked to her man about putting her on the block to hold some shit down and maybe watch over the boys.

Cola was getting money hungry and wanted more. Daddy B wasn't trying to hear her so he agree to give her some extra money. Cola wasn't trying to hear him, she told him either he help her or she would find her own way.

Daddy B went along with Cola's plan to shut her up. He mentioned in their conversation that he wanted to set up shop out west and that this nigga named WaVon had taken over out there and now it was his time to get knocked off the west side. Daddy B chuckled, "I know that nigga like the back of my hands". "My ex Sabrina was messing with that chump while she was dating me, I know that nigga's every move better than he does". Daddy B started to laugh even harder, "then this bitch had the nerve to stop fucking with me because I was fucking her sister Peaches and Peaches stop fucking with me because I was fucking her roommate Cream".

"Mr. big Dick Daddy B passing around that dope dick huh" Cola said. "This ain't no dope dick shorty". Then out of no where Daddy B got mad.

He said "WaVon got a death warrant whenever I see him, that nigga shot my homeboy Gerald, and his boys Prince and Darnell".

"Darnell" Cola shouted "did they go by Dee, Pee and Gee". "Hell yeah" Daddy B shouted "you know those nigga's". "Yeah I had met them through Peaches, it's a long ass story, do you still talk to Peaches"? "Yeah sometimes" Daddy B said. "I would love to talk to her" Cola said, "do you still have her number".

Bogus Azz Hood Chick/ PattiCake Taylor 77

As Daddy B looked through his phone Cola all of sudden snapped, "hold the fuck up" she said, "why the fuck you still got Peaches number in your phone, while you fucking me"? "Cola" he yelled "don't fucking go there, I don't want that bitch". "I'm with you and only you and besides she was way before your time that's why her number still in my phone". Cola kept going on and when Daddy B was tired of her bumping her gums he told her to shut the fuck up! "I don't want to hear that shit" he said "I didn't give you the third degree about that baby not being mine". Cola stood there in shock, looking dumb founded.

"Yeah" he said, "it's just now going on three months since I started dicking you down or did you forget how to add and keep track of who you fucking"?

"Hell nawl nigga, I didn't forget how to count". "You should know that since I count your muther fucking money real well". "As a matter of fact I count it so well that you busting other nigga's shit over it" Cola spat.

Bogus Azz Hood Chick/ PattiCake Taylor 78

"Bitch"! Daddy B slapped the shit out of Cola. "You dumb bitch what the fuck did you say" Daddy B was now heated. Cola stood there with her left hand on her hip and her right hand on her face where Daddy B slapped her.

"How the fuck you think I been flossing like I do"! "Top of the line baby, courtesy of Daddy B". "Deaf couldn't do shit with that chump change you thought was something that you was giving me". "Five hundred dollars a week ain't shit, I can go sell my hella fye ass pussy and make that" said Cola!

"In yours dreams bitch, you better be glad I ain't no woman beater or I would be beating your trifling ass, now get your dusty ass off my block" Daddy B yelled. "Nigga I ain't going no where". "Make me go, you a big bad wolf" Cola yelled back. Daddy B took out his cell phone and made a call.

A few minutes later three females walked up. "What's up baby" this high yellow bitch said to him. Cola was now on fire, everybody knew Cola couldn't stand light skinned girls. "Yo-Yo" Daddy B said "let this stank hoe bitch know the business".

Bogus Azz Hood Chick/ PattiCake Taylor 79

"She been stealing from me had me cracking nigga's heads over my muther fucking paper and she's the bitch that's been stealing". "Hell yeah bitch" said Yolanda better known as Yo-Yo "your time is up". "I've been waiting on your black tar baby ass to fuck up". "Daddy B been turning all this down for you bitch, what a muther fucking waste of his time". "You're old news bitch and I'm the FUCKING new so I would advise your ugly ass to hit the curb and keep it trucking". Cola stood there heated because this was the second high yellow bitch to come and steal her man. Cola went into her bra pulled out a box cutter and went for Yo-Yo's face.

All hell broke loose when A'more Yo-Yo sister jumped in to help her. After Cola took a beating Daddy B finally told them to stop because he did have feelings for the bitch.

Cola was in the hospital a few weeks. While she was there she thought a lot and made a huge mental note to get Daddy B back. It was gonna be poping like popcorn, he would indeed pay for his actions.

Bogus Azz Hood Chick/ PattiCake Taylor 79

Cola was laid up in her bed trying to come up with a plan to get Daddy B. "yes yes I got it" Cola screamed out in pain. "OUCH" Cola said. "Gat damn I got it, I'm gonna find WaVon and tell him the business". "It shouldn't be that hard to find him, I know someone will talk for a few dollars".

Cola was getting herself ready to go out west. After two busses and a train Cola was on the best side of Chicago, the west side.

Cola hit eight blocks before someone finally told her where WaVon was. When Cola hit the next block she was told to look for the black SUV truck with the plates P.T 1 MIL.

Bogus Azz Hood Chick/ PattiCake Taylor 80

You will know when it's him Cola was told. K~Town was the area out west that WaVon was supposed to be running. Cola spotted the truck but no WaVon so she walked up to the dude that was standing by the truck thinking maybe it was his body guard or somebody. Cola said under her breath as she walked closer "damn he's fine", "built up like a model out the magazine". "He's making my pussy hot" Cola smiled at the thought.

"Excuse me", Cola said as he turned around with a smile. "What's up baby" he asked? "Do I know you" Cola said? "The question is do I know you" he said. Cola's mouth flew open, his voice was the same but his looks were way different. "What the hell" Cola yelled out, "you had a face lift or something". "Yeah" he said "I had plastic surgery". "Some shit went down a few years ago and I was on the run for a while". "But now I'm back in full effect". "So what's the deal I heard you was looking for me". He said "Damn" Cola laughed, "it's been a few minutes since I asked somebody about your ass, how you

Bogus Azz Hood Chick/ PattiCake Taylor 81

know so quick"?

"I know everything" he responded back. "Well WaVon" Cola started saying, he cut her off in mid sentence. "WaVon is no longer my name call me P.T or Pretty Tony" he said. Cola busted out laughing gripping her stomach, "whatever" she said. "Anyway do you know this nigga name Daddy B from the low end, 35th and Lowe" to be exact.

Pretty Tony's eyes lit up, "hell yeah that muther fucker is dead when I see him". "I heard that bitch nigga put a hit out on me".

"Yeah, he did" Cola said. "I was kicking it with him for a minute and he was plotting on how to take you down". "He was telling me all types of shit Pretty Tony I asked this nigga to give me a job because his funds wasn't long enough and he told me that he was gonna set up shop out west and use me for bait". "When I said no I wasn't gonna set you up he had his new bitch and crew jumped me and put me in the hospital" Cola said as she lied.

Bogus Azz Hood Chick/ PattiCake Taylor 82

"Later for that nigga" Pretty Tony said, "I'm gonna kill his ass when I see him". "Now back to you, you want a job huh"? "I'll give you one, suck my dick and you will be paid".

"Nigga please" Cola spat, "do I even look like one of your bitches"? "Beside I didn't suck your dick when you was fucking me at eleven". "You was the first nigga to hit this pussy and pop my oh so sweet cherry so I know you can do better then that with your nasty molesting ass".

"Aiight" Pretty Tony said, "I got these four bitches that I send out to do escorts and shit like that". "You can handle those bitches any way you like just make sure my money on point and you will be the youngest bitch on my team making money". "WaVon don't call me no bitch"! "I ain't no bitch, I'm on your team to check your stupid bitches you feel me". "BAM"! said Cola.

"Bitch", didn't I tell you my name is Pretty Tony. "Whatever" Cola said, "Ugly Tony she laughed".

"Now where the hoes at" Cola asked still laughing.

Bogus Azz Hood Chick/ PattiCake Taylor 83

Pretty Tony shook his head at Cola. "They went out on a few calls". Pretty Tony told Cola to take his beeper and the keys to his Chevy and to get up with him later for a meeting at his house. "Okay" Cola said and headed back to the crib. Cola was glad that Daddy B taught her how to drive.

Cola wanted to take a good hot bath and relax before Pretty Tony hit her up to come over. When Cola got home Marilyn stood there with her hands on her hips and told Cola she can begin to pack up her shit, because she would be moving in a week. "No one and I mean no one Marilyn said with a high pitch voice wants teenagers". "I tried to give you a good home but I see you are out to do your own thing". "When you leave here next week you will be off to a group home". "I wish your nappy headed ass the best". "Good night" Marilyn said and walked away.

Pretty Tony didn't page Cola until three days later. Cola was pissed that he took so long but still she wrote all the info down.

Pretty Tony had a three bedroom condo in downtown

Bogus Azz Hood Chick/ PattiCake Taylor 84

Chicago. "It costs money to live down there and Pretty Tony must have money" Cola said to herself. Cola began to get ready, it was kinda chilly out so she put on some super tight jeans. They looked like they were painted on. Cola threw on a fitted shirt and her riding boots. You weren't shit if you didn't have at least one pair of riding boots and an OPP puffy jacket.

Cola valet parked Pretty Tony's Chevy as she entered his building and asked the doorman for unit 2013. "Mr. P.T" the doorman asked? "Yes" Cola replied back. The doorman stepped aside and let Cola up.

As soon as Cola entered Pretty Tony's condo she screamed, "oh my gosh, what the hell you doing here Peaches". "We work for Pretty Tony" Peaches said. There was Peaches along with her side kick Cream and two others, Strawberry and Melon. Peaches yelled to Cream "look who's here, it's Cherri". Cream ran up to Cherri and hugged her along with Peaches.

Strawberry and Melon looked a little upset because they weren't in on the hug.

Bogus Azz Hood Chick/ PattiCake Taylor 85

Peaches noticed the look on their faces so she went over and kissed Strawberry so softly on the lips. Peaches then said "baby this is our friend Cherri", Cola said "what's up" but Strawberry just stared at her with a frown on her face. Cola got an attitude and said "look bitch, frown up if you want to but I'm the new head boss bitch so get your shit in order before I slap some sense into you". Cream jumped up and said "WHAT".. "What you mean" Cherri? "What the fuck you think it mean" Cream, "did I 'muther fucking' bite my tongue". Cola screamed.

"Hell nawl I didn't, I got the power to set you bitches straight so if you want to be treated like women you need to start acting as such or I'll just treat you like hoe's and trick's". "I got the juice, remember that"! "Speaking of juices, Strawberry if you don't get that ugly ass frown off your face I'm gonna make you get on your damn knees with those big old lips and suck my pussy, I already can't stand light skinned bitches". "Matter of fact" Cola said in a loud tone "Come suck my pussy and you better make me cum".

Bogus Azz Hood Chick/ PattiCake Taylor 86

Cola was loving the action. Cream and the other girls were heated. Cream whispered "where the hell Pretty Tony go"? Speaking of the devil Pretty Tony entered and Strawberry jumped up. That made Cola mad. "Bitch don't stop now, the show ain't over because Pretty Tony is here"! "You better make me cum and make me cum now hoe"! Cola said. Cola cum all in Strawberry's mouth and when she was done she took a shower put on one of Pretty Tony over size T-shirt and then founded out what the business at hand was.

Pretty Tony informed the girls that Cola was in charge. "Who the hell is Cola" Cream asked? "Me bitch" Cola answered, "I know you didn't think my real name was Cherri". Cola started to laugh, "please tell me your real name isn't Cream". Cream said "hell nawl"! "Ok then dumb bitch" Cola shook her head. Cola looked over to Pretty Tony and said "Peaches and Cream know me as Cherri, long ass story but Peaches save me". So Peaches can be my understudy in case I need her.

Pretty Tony gave Cola a cell phone, and told her the number

Bogus Azz Hood Chick/ PattiCake Taylor 87

was 555-FUCK. "How nice" Cola said with a grin. The phone rang and Cola answer: "Hello this is Split Pussy how may I help you"? All heads and eye balls turned and looked Cola's way.

All they heard Cola say is yes and that will be six hundred dollars. What's the address? We will be there. "Click"!

Pretty Tony looked over at Cola and asked her what that was all about. Cola explained it was a new client and he wanted a girl on girl and for six hundred dollars I'm going to do that shit. "My play mate of choice will be the one and only Strawberry, she can eat a mean pussy"! "Now bitch go get dressed" Cola said to her.

Strawberry did as she was told. The other ladies just continued to look at Cola as Pretty Tony was hitting Cola from the back. She moaned and he talked. As he moaned he banged her harder and harder until he came thinking about that virgin pussy Cola once had. When Pretty Tony was done he said "I'm gonna bang Daddy B the same way, just not with my dick"!

Bogus Azz Hood Chick/ PattiCake Taylor 88

An hour later Cola and Strawberry arrived at Mr. Dick's house. Mr. Dick is what he called himself over the phone. When Cola got there she told Mr. Dick her name was Spicy. As he opened the door further Cola noticed he had it all laid out. Rose petals, Cristal, Shrimp cocktails and Lobster. "What the hell was he thinking" Cola thought, this was only supposed to be a threesome. It just didn't feel right to Cola.

Cola knew nothing about the lifestyle and had not done it before but one thing she did know was that it was only a fuck. Cola looked over to Strawberry and said bring your ass this don't feel right. Strawberry refused and told Cola she could leave if she wanted too "I'm staying" Strawberry said, "I'm gonna make my money". "Aiight bitch go to jail" Cola stated. "Nawl fuck that, bring your ass and bring it now or I'm gonna call Pretty Tony and your ass gonna be grass" Cola yelled. "Do what you gotta do" Strawberry said. Cola went up to Strawberry and slapped the shit out of her, "that's for being disrespectful hoe and trying to act hard" said Cola.

Bogus Azz Hood Chick/ PattiCake Taylor 89

Cola was leaving, It seem like all eyes were on her. Cola continue to walk and all she heard was freeze "this is the police put your hands and don't move". Cola did just that as she tried to hold her pee! Cola turned to face the police when she saw this dude face down on the ground in handcuffs. Cola exhaled she thought the police were there for her.

In the blink of an eye she knew that lifestyle wasn't for her and she wanted out. Cola hit Pretty Tony's cell phone as she waited for a cab, she informed him about Strawberry and that she wanted out as well.

Pretty Tony was pissed as he lashed out at Cola. "I knew you was too young for this grown woman shit" he told her. "But I still need your help in taking down Daddy B".

"Okay" Cola said. Since the cab was taking forever Cola decided to walk and feel the light breeze. As Cola was walking down the street some dude was trying to holla. "A shorty what's your name" dude asked. "Rayn" Cola said. "RAYN" he repeated sounding surprise.

Bogus Azz Hood Chick/ PattiCake Taylor 90

"Yeah is there a problem with my name or something" Cola said with a frown. "Damn baby no need to frown, you too pretty for that". "I'm Treez because I get high, high, HIGH, he chuckled and said how can a nigga get to know you, can I take you to the movies"? "Maybe some other time" Cola said, "I'm tired, my feet hurt and I'm just trying to get home". "I'll take you" Treez said.

Cola thought for a minute, "damn where is that fucking cab". "Ummmm, I don't get in cars with stranger's" Cola said. "Baby I'm not gonna hurt ya, just trying to help a fine sista like yourself out" Treez responded. Cola thought about it for a second and then went for the ride. They small talked for a minute and then Treez pulled up in a alley. When Cola asked why, he said he had to piss. The next thing Cola knew she was looking at a gun in her face. Treez force Cola to suck his dick, he nutted in her mouth like she was a whore on the street and when he was done he put her out his car and drove off. Cola stood there looking stupid , spitting and coughing.

Bogus Azz Hood Chick/ PattiCake Taylor 91

Cola walked home pissed that she didn't drive and mad that she didn't wait for her cab.

"Where is my life headed" Cola asked herself. "My momma a drunk who didn't want me, my fucking granny gave up on me too, shaking my damn head at my supposed to be family". "I'm so tired of my fucking life, I should just kill myself, the thought quickly came to her".

Cola's mind was in a daze, wondering why she had been dealt a bullshit hand in life. Living day by day trying to be someone else other than…. Cola Krown Blue Royalty Johnson, "maybe that's why I keep using all these fake names" Cola began to cry, "trying to be someone I'm not". "Damn I must really be ashamed of who I am". Cola cried herself to sleep. She had two more days before she was headed to the group home.

The next morning Cola decided to stay in all day to get her thoughts together. All day Cola's foster mother Marilyn wondered why Cola hadn't come out of her room.

Bogus Azz Hood Chick/ PattiCake Taylor 92

Marilyn knocked on the door, in a fear that Cola had done something crazy. Cola screamed at the top of her lungs to leave her alone. Marilyn asked Cola to unlock the door. Cola didn't say anything at first, all the sudden Marilyn heard Cola making these funny noises. Marilyn ran to call Mr. Williams, Cola's case worker. Mr. Williams arrived with a therapist and a paramedic.

When Mr. Williams banged on Cola's bedroom door Cola began to gag. Cola revealed that she had drank a gallon of bleach. Cola over heard them talking on the outside the door. Their dumbass believed that she had actually tried to kill herself. They started trying to kick her bedroom door down. When they finally got the door down Cola ran to the window as if she was about to jump out.

Marilyn grabbed Cola by her shirt and pulled her back in. The paramedic put Cola in a straight jacket and took her to a behavior center for youths. The crazy ward for kids Cola called it. Things seemed to be going downhill for Cola.

Bogus Azz Hood Chick/ PattiCake Taylor 93

Cola really tried to harm herself this time. Cola tied a long sleeve shirt on the bathroom door and the other part around her neck, she then slammed the bathroom door as hard as she could trying to choke herself. As she continued a staff member heard the noise.

Once the staff member saw what Cola was doing she called code blue. They used code blue for assistance when a patient was trying to harm themselves. They ran in and put Cola in another straight jacket, she kicked and screamed and it took five staff members to help. They all began to call her crazy, so Cola showed them crazy.

They had to hold her down to dope her up with medication. they placed Cola in a small room by herself. The next morning Cola started kicking the door of the room that they had placed her in like she was crazy. They refused to let her out until she calmed down. After a week of medication, eating alone and a using a sink to wash up in Cola decided to get her shit together or so they thought.

Bogus Azz Hood Chick/ PattiCake Taylor 94

Cola did as she was told, she wanted to get off level one and get to level five so she could go outside. Level one was for all the bad patients and the staff had to watch them around the clock. Level five was for the good ones, they got freedom to do whatever they wanted.

After a few weeks Cola was on level three which was good, it meant she was improving. Cola befriended a white girl named Sara. Sara and Cola became very close since they were on the same level and was able to go to the cafeteria to eat lunch together. They would trade stories about life. Sara was in the center because she tried to kill her boyfriend when he blacked her eye one too many times. The staff was dumb as hell why would they put Sara and Cola in the same room together. Did they forget Cola tried to commit suicide and Sara could have had a homicide case if her boyfriend had pressed chargers or even died. As Cola laid in her bunk with lots of thoughts, she couldn't wait to reach level five to go outside so she could runaway.

Bogus Azz Hood Chick/ PattiCake Taylor 95

Cola was ready to leave that center, she had to do a lot to keep the staff off her back and Cola wasn't happy with it. Just as Cola was in deep thought she was called to the front desk.

Mr. Avery the staff supervisor informed her that she had a visitor in the visitor's room. Cola went into the visitor's room and when she walked in all she could do was cry.

Cola saw her mom Marlene and her Grandma Lynda. Cola ran up to them both and hugged them tight. "I see" she said through sobs, "I see you both really do care about me"!

Marlene told her baby girl that she was on the right track and was getting her life together so that she could come home. Cola smiled as tears flowed through her beautiful bold brown eyes.

When Cola saw the big bag of goodies that Lynda and Marlene brought for her she stopped crying so she could see what all she had. Just the thought of Cola going home made her really want to be good now.

Three weeks later Cola was discharged but she ended up in a group home.

Bogus Azz Hood Chick/ PattiCake Taylor 96

Cola was informed that there was a foster mother willing to take her in, but Ms. House was out of town and that she had to wait another couple weeks before she could move into her new home.

Two months later Cola moved in with the House family. Ms. House had six grown daughters and to Cola's surprise they were nice to her and treated her as if she was there real sister. All Cola ever wanted was for someone to love her and show her love. Everything was going good.

Cola was about to turn eighteen years old. Time had flown by so quickly and she had a decision to make. Marlene had finally gotten her shit together but by that time the state was offering Cola an independent living program where she would have her own apartment. They paid her rent, give her an allowance and took care of everything until she was twenty one years old.

Cola had chosen to stay in the system and Marlene was pissed the fuck off.

Bogus Azz Hood Chick/ PattiCake Taylor 97

Cola didn't care what the hell Marlene thought. "I'd rather be on my own then have to deal with a drunk, I mean recovering AA dot drunk dot com mother" Cola mumbled.

The only huge rule to the program was that you couldn't have a man living with you. That was cool as far as Cola was concerned, little did they know Cola didn't want a man any more. On those lonely nights in the behavior center Cola would crawl in bed with Sara. Sara held her tight and one thing lead to another and Sara became gay for the stay, and when Cola left she was straight again.

Cola had that feeling that just wouldn't go away despite hearing that being a lesbian was wrong and not of god. "HA" Cola said aloud, "if that's the case no one sin is greater then the other, I swear people act like you got a STD when you mention same sex relationships".

Cola was so on ten to move that she took the first apartment that she could find within the program. Cola founded an apartment on the south side of Chicago.

Bogus Azz Hood Chick/ PattiCake Taylor 98

She was ready to move and have her own shit. Everything was great Cola even befriended some new people Felicia {Fee} and Tasha {Tay}. Tay was this boyish looking girl and Fee was the girly looking one, they were lesbians lovers. When Fee asked Cola what her name was, Cola responded the only way she seemed to know how by changing her name. "My name is Almond" Cola said with a slight grin. Almond and Fee became real cool. Fee was taking Cola to all the gay spots. Fee was very well known so they didn't need no I.D and Cola was loving every moment of it. Fee took Cola to a hole in the wall club on 63rd and King Drive called Girl on Girl, Cola was amazed.

It's mad crazy up in here Cola thought to herself, all the girly looking girls was with boyish looking girls. "What the fuck is the point of being with a woman if your woman looks like a man, thinks she a man, smells like a man ewwww"! "Hell I might as well stick with a man". Cola knew right off back she wanted to be with a girly woman from head to toe that had

Bogus Azz Hood Chick/ PattiCake Taylor 99

a body just like hers, short and thick with ass.

Cola spotted a fine sexy woman in the corner dancing in the mirror. Cola thought for a minute, "what the hell do you say to a female". Cola walked up to the woman and stared for a second before saying "hey sweetie, what's your name"? The female looked and then laughed in Cola's face. Cola was heated. "What the fuck you laughing at" Cola screamed through the music. "Who the fuck are you" the female yelled back.

"I'm muther fucking Cola, I mean Almond bitch". "I was trying to give you a compliment about your beauty, but I see your ass is acting all snotty about your name and shit so fuck you".

Cola turned around to walk away, when the female said wait, "my name is Adore". "It was just funny to see a fem looking woman like yourself trying to holla but I see you are aggressive and I like that" Adore said. Cola smiled then said "don't get it twisted because it's not my outer appearance that makes me aggressive, it's me Cola Krown Blue Royalty Johnson".

Bogus Azz Hood Chick/ PattiCake Taylor 100

"Who" Adore asked.

"Never mind" Cola said! Cola wanted to show Adore who was in charge so she grabbed a hand full of Adore's weave and began to tongue her down. When they were done Cola told Adore to give up them seven digits and Adore did just that.

It was closing time at the club, Fee yelled over to Cola to head to the car, out of no were Fee just started laughing then Cola starting laughing too. She asked Fee what the joke was all about! "Damn Almond" Fee said still laughing, "I wish I had met you hella early because you mad crazy, I like how you took control".

Cola laughed to herself as Fee talked with that big ass gap in her mouth. That was another one of Cola's pet peeves, light skinned hoes and gaps between the teeth. Fee was alright looking, carmel skin, a little chubby and this big huge gap in her mouth like it used to be a tooth there or something.

Later that evening Cola called Adore. They had a great

Bogus Azz Hood Chick/ PattiCake Taylor 101

conversation, a little different from most but it was all good in Cola eyes. Cola was feeling Adore already. Adore was fly, she had a stripper body and a pretty face. Thinking of strippers made Cola think of Peaches and Cream, and most of all Strawberry as she laughed at the thought.

"Damn" Cola said, "I need some money". "Guess I'm gonna be a stripper hell I got a cola shaped body". "The state done gave me a crib and I ain't got shit in it, no job, no nothing". Cola blew out air at the thought. "I guess when I get up in the A.M I'll go to The Pole in the wall and use the gift God gave me". Cola said her prayers for the first time in a long time then turned over and went to sleep. Cola was in a deep dream, all she could hear was ass, ass, ass can I get a lap dance Almond nut, can I nut on you. Cola jumped up out of her sleep trying to shake that shit off.

The next morning Cola got super fly. She headed to The Pole in the wall in some fly shit she had never heard of before. Some of the guys in the hood had hit a freight train and as they

Bogus Azz Hood Chick/ PattiCake Taylor 102

was dropping shit Cola was picking it up. Cola finally got to the club and asked the girl at the desk for the owner. "Do you have an appointment" the ugly girl asked. "No I don't" Cola said with an attitude. "Well the owner is not here and you need to make an appointment to see him anyway" the girl said.

The receptionist was lying, she was just hating on Cola body. She was very unattractive and she had scars from being hit in the face with a bottle and she looked like she hadn't eaten in years. Cola said "whatever bitch" and rolled her eyes. She walked out the door and some dude said "damn girl what your name"?

"ALMOND" Cola yelled "who the fuck wants to know"? "First of all young lady you should not be talking in that type of manner, I am the owner T.P". Cola said shit under her breath as she stared at the girl behind the desk. Cola wanted to punch her in the face for lying and saying the owner wasn't there. Cola turned around and said "I'm sorry Mr. T.P"

'It's just that ugly ass girl you got working for you said you weren't here with her hating ass". "Almond that's your name correct"? he said. "Yes" Cola said. "That ugly young lady happens to be my daughter" he said. "I see you are a very out spoken young lady but working here you gonna have to put a muzzle on your mouth" T.P said. Cola mouth flew open, "I'm sorry but she gave me lots of attitude and I didn't even do anything to her other than ask was the owner here". Cola said

"Well" T.P said "I'll look over it this time, how may I help you"?

"Well sir my name is Cola but everybody calls me Almond I'm in need of some part time work". "As you can see I'm a ten plus on the scale but I wouldn't say I'm a dime because I'm too fine to be change".

T.P just started laughing and licking his lips. "Well Ms. Almond can you dance"? Cola said "yeah you want to see". T.P's eyes lit up and then he said "meet me in the back so I can see what you working with".

Cola entered the small room with a small stage and a pole.

Bogus Azz Hood Chick/ PattiCake Taylor 104

Cola closed her eyes and went for what she knew. All the years of dancing in the mirror and playing with herself paid off. She was hoping that she would impress Mr. T.P as he looked at her and said "act like I'm a customer and give me a lap dance". When Cola started giving T.P a dance and a blow job, he said "you're HIRED". "What is the stage name you want to go by"?

Cola thought for a few seconds as she thought about all the names she used over the years. She smiled then said "Lolli~Pop". "Oh yeah" T.P said with a grin "when you want to start"? Cola told him she would get back with him. She couldn't wait to start to be the new money maker in the club. Cola needed some money and she needed it now. Cola left The Pole in the Wall and headed to the bus stop just then she noticed some dude driving a fly ass car. Dude seen Cola looking so he trailed her until she stopped.

"Hey chocolate girl what's your name"?. Cola thought for a min "damn I always meet these dusty ass nigga's walking I need a car of my own".

Bogus Azz Hood Chick/ PattiCake Taylor 105

"First of all" she said, "my name ain't chocolate girl". "Damn" he said, "can a brother holla at a fine sista like yourself". "Well" Cola said with a slight attitude "can a real brother get his lazy ass out the car". "I ain't no hoe I guess you want to see my ass all up in the air like a hood rat trying to talk to you".

"Now if you really want to holla you need to get out your car" Cola shouted.

The dude told Cola that she had a smart ass mouth but he was liking her being sassy. Cola waved her hand at him and started to walk to another bus stop. "Aye baby girl, wait a second" he said as he got out his car and jogged to catch up with Cola. "You got just a little too much attitude baby girl". "My name ain't baby girl, it's Lolli~Pop" Cola replied. He laughed and then said "my name was Maine". Maine tried to offer Cola a ride but she quickly said no.

He asked for her number but she told him that she had just moved and didn't have a phone. Maybe I'll see you again if it's

Bogus Azz Hood Chick/ PattiCake Taylor 106

meant to be Cola told him. It's meant to be right now he said, here's mine. Cola took his number, he had already written it down, probably for some other girl. Cola got on the bus finally to head home.

Cola finally got around the crib, as she walked up the block she saw Fee.

"What up" Fee, Cola said to her. "Hey Almond what's up" Fee replied. "Shit" Cola responded.

"Giiiirl" Fee said, "I got some Jodeci tickets". "Do you want to go to the concert with me and hear K.C say Oooooh yeah" Fee laughed out loud. "Hell yeah" Cola said "his ass be begging too just like Keith Sweat". "When is the concert Fee"? asked Cola "Tonight", Fee said, "Sorry for the short notice but my girl got me these tickets and told me to take someone and have fun, so I chose you Almond". "It's all good" Cola said.

"Well gat damn it, let's get this party started right" Fee said. They both laughed and started toward there unit. Fee told Cola that she would be ready at seven. "Alright" Cola yelled, "I

Bogus Azz Hood Chick/ PattiCake Taylor 107

guess I won't be going to work tonight, I'm going to see Jodeci and special guest Keith Sweat begging ass". "You may be young but you ready, ready to learn" Cola hum to herself.

With everything going on Cola had forgotten all about Adore. Cola got in the house, pulled out her some outfits, pinned her hair up and took a nice bath. Then she called Adore. As the phone rung Cola thought what would they talk about. Ring, ring, ring.

Cola was just about to hang up when a male voice answered the phone. "Hello" he said. "Oh I'm sorry" Cola said "may I speak with Adore". "Who this" he asked. "This Cola her friend". "Adore don't have no friends".. "click". "No this muther fucker didn't hang up in my face" Cola said to herself, "Oh well fuck it". "I gotta get ready for this concert". Cola got dressed and waited for Fee to show up.

Just when she was about to use the bathroom. Fee rang the doorbell. Cola spoke through the intercom and told Fee she was coming down. Cola walked very slowly down the stairs in her 5

Bogus Azz Hood Chick/ PattiCake Taylor 108

inch payless specials. Cola eyes lit up when she saw the long white limo. As Fee and Cola entered the limo, Cola noticed Fee's boy looking friend Tasha and some other boy looking girl, Fee said her name was Smoove.

Now Smoove was fiiiiiiiine then a muther but damn why she had to be light skinned Cola thought.

"What up everybody" Cola said after coming out of her thoughts. They were cruising down Stoney Island going to The Regal Theater where the concert was.

Smoove begin to asked Cola one in a million questions. Cola's mind went blank, she couldn't believe how fine Smoove was to be a female. They pulled up in front of the Regal in there white stretch limo as if they were K.C and Jo-Jo themselves. Almond, "ALMOND" Fee said again as she hit Cola on the leg to get her attention.

"Girl where the hell is your mind at"? Cola just shook her head and said "I was in never, never land" she started laughing.

At about 11pm the concert was over, they all hopped back

in the limo and decided to go to an all night diner to get something to eat.

Smoove finally asked Cola for her number. Cola was trying to play hard to get, but she finally gave in when Smoove said "you cute and all but I don't sweat bitches".

Smoove was finer than any real man Cola had ever seen and for her to be a girl, "OMG", Cola said to herself. Cola was all smiles the next day when she received the call from Smoove. She rushed off the phone with Adore to talk to her.

Adore was trying to explain that the dude that answered the phone when Cola called the night before was her brother. Cola responded with a "yeah right" and then clicked back over to talk to Smoove. Smoove was talking some shit to Cola, after being on the phone for a hour Smoove was knocking on Cola's door twenty minutes later.

Cola came to the door butt naked and ready to do whatever. Smoove didn't waste no time, she knew what the business was. Smoove was tonguing Cola down like no other. Smoove flipped

Bogus Azz Hood Chick/ PattiCake Taylor 110

Cola on her stomach. Cola mind wondered off as Smoove licked her neck, down her back and even her booty crack. Cola moaned so softly as Smoove massaged her shoulders and worked her way back down her fat ass. Smoove massaged her booty then licked it and licked it again. She worked her way down Cola legs massaging her feet, licking and sucking her toes. Smoove sucked Cola toe's as if she was singing this little piggy went to the market.

    Smoove flipped Cola over and up her legs went. Smoove missed her pussy and went straight for her breast as her nipples stood up right at attention. Smoove kissed so gently working her way back down to Cola navel and then she reached the spot. Cola smiled as Smoove admired her heart shape pussy. "Oh, Oh what the hell you doing to me" Cola asked as Smoove went in and out then circled around her clit with her tongue.

    Cola was feeling real good, so damn good that she flip Smoove ass over so she could do the same thing. Although Cola never ate pussy before she was going to try her best.

Bogus Azz Hood Chick/ PattiCake Taylor 111

As Cola flicked her tongue really fast around Smoove's neck working her way down Smoove pushed her away and said, "I don't like to receive oral sex I'm a touch me not".

"What"!! Cola yelled, "what the fuck is a TOUCH ME NOT"? "Any real nigga wants his dick sucked".

Smoove said "exactly" and pulled out some long dildo attach to her from her waist. Cola laughed and told Smoove to get the fuck out her crib. "Fuck I look like sucking on plastic" Cola said as she slammed her door. At that moment Cola knew butch studs wasn't for her. From now on Cola would only date women who looked like women.

Cola couldn't understand why women wanted to look, smell, dress, and talk like nigga's anyways. "I'm gonna get me a thick chick, no lighter then carmel skin". Cola just shook her head as she headed to the shower, when she was done she went to bed.

The next morning Cola woke up to screaming from the neighbor's kids playing in the hallway. Cola was pissed. "Omg, glad I don't have no fucking kids" she said to herself.

Bogus Azz Hood Chick/ PattiCake Taylor 112

It was gonna be a boring day so Cola decided she was gonna go up on Madison to do a little window shopping so when she came up on some money she would already know what she wanted. Madison and Pulaski was a little hood mall and everybody went there like it was Beverly Hills or something.

Cola got ready and headed to the bus stop. She made it just in time to get the bus. There were a group of girls loud talking and acting stupid, Cola just shook her head at the nonsense but then something caught her attention when one of the girls said something about a gay party line called "The Under L". Before Cola got off the bus she asked if she could get the number. The girl gave it to her.

Later that evening Cola called the party line to be nosy. It was so much going on that Cola got excited. She left a message on something call the B-board with a box number where she could be reached, if someone was digging her they could leave her a message.

Cola fell asleep while she was on the party line and went into a dream about her life. "Why me, why me, why does no one love me, who am I, I'm so tired of my life" Cola tossed and turned into her dream. "Hello", Hell~ooooooo, Cola jumped up out her sleep and said "Hello". "Hey who this"? the girl on the other end said.

This um Cola paused for a minute and said damn what name I'm I gonna use now. "Damn, fuck it"! "I'm so tired of using different names and shit, maybe for once I'll just use my real name". "This Cola who this"? This is "Sweet Candy" the girl said. Cola laughed and then said "hey Sweet". Cola and Sweet talked in a private one on one room for about a hour just getting to know each other a little bit. Cola was blown away and wanted to know what the deal was with this chick who called herself Sweet Candy, she never had been with a woman before. Cola and Sweet exchanged numbers. The next day Cola decided to call Sweet since Sweet hadn't called her.

As they talked Sweet wanted to know how many girls Cola had been with and if she had been to the doctor to get checked.

Bogus Azz Hood Chick/ PattiCake Taylor 114

Cola said she had been with a few women but they only had oral sex with her. Cola suggested that if they were gonna be intimate that they could go to the doctor together to be checked out and tested for any sexually transmitted diseases.

"No worries though I'm good" Cola said "and if we ever have sex, I'm sure I can do better then them fools can". "I know how I like to be touched and feel inside".

Sweet Candy was out of town so Cola made a mental note when she came home to handle some bedroom business with her if she was fly. As they said goodbye Cola gave Sweet Candy her number again just in case she wanted to call sooner. With a name like that Cola thought, "she better taste just like that, sweet candy". "Call me when you hit Chicago lil momma" Cola said. Sweet Candy couldn't wait to talk to Cola again, she hit Cola the next day. They stayed on the phone almost all day. About a month later…

They were meeting each other for the first time. They made plans to meet on 95th and the Dan Ryan.

Bogus Azz Hood Chick/ PattiCake Taylor 115

Cola had a flashed back to when she was left on the Dan Ryan in nothing but a sheet but she didn't let that stop her from going to see this Sweet Candy chick. Cola had completely changed her look. She told Sweet Candy to look for someone with a short Anita Baker haircut, baggy jeans and a plaid shirt. Cola had done a 360, she now looked boyish.

As Cola was coming off the escalator she spotted Sweet Candy right away. "Dammmmn", "she was a fine, pretty dark skinned sister 5'1 about 130lbs long hair and thick in all the right places". "She had to be every man's dream" Cola mumble. They headed to Sweet Candy's crib where they kicked it for a while. Sweet Candy lived with her O.G so Cola asked when she was gonna come to her crib. Cola was on some thirsty type of shit, she wanted to get in between them Sweet Candy thighs. Sweet Candy's reply was now. "That's what I'm talking about" Cola said.

Sweet Candy asked her mom if she could use her car. They were at Cola's crib in no time. Cola pretty much took control

Bogus Azz Hood Chick/ PattiCake Taylor 116

and that's what Sweet Candy wanted. When Cola took off Sweet Candy's clothes she removed her own and they headed to the shower. When they were done Cola oiled Sweet Candy down with cherry scented lickable lotion. Cola then did things she never knew she could do with a woman. Cola and Sweet Candy was feeling each other real hard, Oh so Cola thought.

After six months of dating Sweet Candy broke Cola's heart. She told Cola that she didn't want to date no more because she wasn't a man and if she was a man everything would be better. Sweet Candy told Cola her mom was being too nosy and she was tired of lying.

Cola was hurt, she was really feeling her some Sweet Candy. Cola hung up from her call with Sweet Candy, took a shower, put some clothes on, and headed to the train all the way to the west side to the circle just to chill.

Cola went and got her some weed and some Krown Blue Royal to drink. Cola wasn't really a drinker or smoker but she needed something to take the pain away. While Cola was at the circle she met some dude named Jamal. Cola thought "what the hell", "might as well fuck with a nigga, shit it's no difference bitches will hurt you too".

The crazy thing was that Cola was shocked he tried to holla at her. She had on shaggy jeans and boxers. "Maybe he thinks I'm a tom boy" Cola laughed it off.

Jamal turned out to be real cool. Cola went back to looking like a woman. Jamal wined and dined her and treated her like a lady, at first Cola thought it was just so he could get some ass but it wasn't. Jamal was hitting Cola so hard with money that she was able to furnish her crib and buy her a used car. Her short hair was hot and Cola's lips were popping on top of that Cola's body was something to die for. She felt like she was finer then most.

The next morning, it was feeling pretty good out.

Cola called Fee and ask her to come out and sit on the front with her. While Cola was sitting on the porch waiting on Fee some ugly dude came up to Cola talking about "thickness with all that lip gloss on your lips, look like you been sucking on a pork chop". Cola got mad and told the dude, "you just mad it ain't your pork chop I'm sucking". Old boy called Cola a bitch and walked off.

Fee met Cola on the front and told her she was getting ready to go to a party. A house party in Oak Park Illinois which was on the border line of the west side of Chicago. "Almond", Fee said you want to roll. "Almond" Fee repeated. Cola frowned, "oh girl yeah you know I'm down". Cola laughed to herself almost forgetting she told Fee her name was Almond. Fee was telling Cola about this girl named Tamesha who could throw some of the chain house parties. Cola busted out and said fat and dark skinned Tamesha. "Yeah" Fee said "you know her". "Hell yeah" Cola said "can't really stand her though she's a fat ass liar, but I'll roll with you.

Fee and Cola finally made it to Tamesha's house. They were all just chilling in the living room when a knock came at the door. It was a fine ass dark skinned nigga at the door.

Bogus Azz Hood Chick/ PattiCake Taylor

Everybody was looking crazy though because the house party was full of dykes. He asked for Tamesha. Tamesha came to the door and just stood there looking dumb founded.

Tamesha said:
"what's up do I know you"? Dude said "oh I'm sorry I'm looking for Tamesha". She said "I am Tamesha", he looked at her and just started laughing. "No" he said "I'm looking for light skinned Tamesha".

Everybody was standing around being nosy. Tamesha said "well I don't know no light skinned Tamesha and how the hell you end up at my house with my address".

Dude pulled out an envelope with her name, address and picture. Tamesha's eyes got big ass hell. She was speechless.

Trigger was some nigga from jail that Tamesha had been writing for five years. She tried to break it off with him before he came home because he was talking about marrying her.

Trigger wasn't trying to hear it, he wanted some Tamesha. Tamesha had sent him a picture of this girl she hung with named Fantasy. Fantasy jumped up from her chair and said "what the fuck". "What the fuck is on your bird Tamesha sending my picture to a nigga in jail, you fat ugly hoe". "You wish you could be me huh bitch, well you ain't and you will never be black stank bitch".

Tamesha went all force on Fantasy knocking her to the floor, and then jumped down on her with all her weight as if she was a wrestler. Some people tried to break it up and other's left. Cola and Fee were laughing there asses off as they headed out the door on their way home.

Cola and Fee were in front of their building when Cola saw a familiar face it was Pretty Tony. "What's up Cherri, I mean Spicy or Cola" Pretty Tony said as he laughed, "damn girl how many damn names do you have"? That's when Fee looked and said "I thought your name was Almond". "It is" Cola said to her "it's my middle name".

"Oh okay" Fee laughed and said "girl gone talk to your friend I'll be back".

Bogus Azz Hood Chick/ PattiCake Taylor 121

Okay" Cola said and turned her attention to Pretty Tony asking him who he knew on her block. He told her he was just in the area, and since he saw her he decided to stop.

Pretty Tony wanted to know if she still wanted to get even with Daddy B. As Cola stood there she started to get bad vibes. Cola told Pretty Tony she would talk to him later about that, she didn't want to discuss that situation outside.

"Okay" he said, they hugged walked their separate ways.

As Pretty Tony was getting back in his truck, A ring of fire came out of no where. Cola felt something through her leg. Cola screamed as she saw Fee stabbing her with an ice pick in her leg. Cola used all her strength to kick Fee in the face with her other leg.

Police came from all directions. Cola was transported to the emergency room, she had lost a lot of blood but she would be okay.

A few days later Cola founded out that Daddy B and Pretty Tony was dead.

Bogus Azz Hood Chick/ PattiCake Taylor 122

That bitch Fee was cool with Daddy B new chick Yo-Yo, she had sent her a picture of Daddy B and Cola from when they were together and Fee was on the look out just in case she happen to run into Cola. How the hell Cola and Fee ended up in the same building Cola had no clue.

Daddy B had killed Pretty Tony during the shoot out between their crews. One of Daddy B main guy's had shot him just for rank. Melo was his name and he wanted to take over the low end but for that to happen Daddy B had to go.

Cola didn't know who she would miss the most, Wavon "Pretty Tony" the man who took her woman hood or Daddy B the man who made her feel like a woman. Fee had moved out the building while Cola was in the hospital.

Cola planned to get that hoe if she ever saw her again, on site she didn't give two fucks. "Shit my leg still hurt's like crazy, I can't wait until I see that hoe", Cola said to herself.

"Damn", Cola shouted this nigga Jamal just came out of no where.

Bogus Azz Hood Chick/ PattiCake Taylor 123

"I haven't seen your ass in week and I don't want to be bothered" Cola said to Jamal. Somehow Jamal heard that Cola got stabbed and when Cola told him to vanish, this nigga tried to bribe her with his money.

Cola wanted it so bad, but she told him to get the fuck out her face. Jamal said your loss bitch and moved around her ass.

On Monday Cola called her caseworker and said she needed to move because of the situation at hand, she didn't feel safe anymore. Cola sat on the floor as if she was a child or something banging the walls and floors saying how fucked up her life was. She was feeling like she should kill herself. "I have, I have" as she cried through her tears, "I have nothing to live for". "I lost my damn job at The Pole in the wall because I was an no show". "Jamal was hitting me off so good, that I didn't need to work". "How dumb was I, what the fuck I'm I gonna do" Cola asked herself. Cola's caseworker came and took her to an apartment they already had on 68th and Perry since there was no time Cola to find another unit on her own.

Bogus Azz Hood Chick/ PattiCake Taylor 124

Cola went into deep thought, "for now on I'm gonna work toward getting my life together and I'm gonna start with loving me and using the name my drunk ass momma gave me Cola Krown Blue Royalty Johnson", Cola chuckled at that thought.

Cola laid down but wasn't feeling good. She got up and took some meds but yet her stomach kept hurting and she was throwing up so she finally went to the county hospital after a week of being sick. She founded out she had Gonorrhea a S-T-D. She was treated with a shot in the ass and some pills, good for her she was treated in time or it could have been worse.

Cola was pissed the fuck off because Jamal had burnt her and she was even more pissed that she called his ass back that night for that money. He fucked her and instead of leaving the money, he left her with an infection.

Cola hurried home so she could get some rest. She had to pack so she could move into her new crib. Cola pulled up in front of her crib and as usual nigga's were outside.

Bogus Azz Hood Chick/ PattiCake Taylor 125

There were some dudes on the block staring at her and laughing. She did look a hot mess so Cola just waved they asses off. Then one of the dude's said "hey you stuck up bi-sexual bitch". Cola kept walking. "I HEARD YOU BURNING BITCH". Cola turned around fast as hell damn near breaking her neck.

"Excuse me nigga" she said, "I don't know where you getting your information but you talking to the wrong bitch". He laughed and said "you can thank my mans Jamal for the info hoe"!

"Jamal", Cola said loudly, "that nigga just mad because I dump his little dick ass after taking all his muther fucking money so next time get your facts right". "Trick ass nigga" Cola said and turned around to go in the house. Cola was glad she was moving in a few days but she was so upset that she cried and cried. "Never again will another muther fucker burn me". Cola showered, cooked her something to eat and popped her first set of pills....

she had to take them for seven days straight.

Two weeks later Cola had gotten settled in her new crib, then her caseworker tells her she needs to find a job or go to school or be kick out the program. Cola was pissed.

There was a McDonald's up the street so Cola got her a job there. She was only making $4.25 an hour but that wasn't shit in Cola's eyes she was pissed so she did what she had to do, she started stealing from the register.

After a year of being with McDonald's Cola had gotten herself fired, for showing this girl named Makala how to steal out the register. When Makala got busted she told on Cola too. Cola had lost her job and gained 35lbs from eating all those burger and fries.

Cola wasn't mad though because it didn't stop her flow of nigga's. Cola had a different nigga for everyday of the week. One dude she was digging real hard named Cozell, he was fine as hell in her eyes. Cola met him at this teen club for the eighteen and over crowd on Madison and Cicero.

Bogus Azz Hood Chick/ PattiCake Taylor 127

She thought he was the flyest from his clothes to his gym shoes. He was a baby drug dealer but looking at him you would have thought he was big time. He spoiled Cola rotten, she wanted for nothing but to come to his crib.

Two months later Cozell had invited Cola over to meet his mom but Cola wasn't no dummy like he thought. She knew he only called her over because he had gotten busted and was on house arrest and he wanted some ass but he couldn't make no moves.

Cola headed to take the bus over to Cozell's house because Jamal had somebody to steal her car when she was in the old neighborhood. Cola knew it was him because he was salty and he knew she bought that car with his money.

After being over Cozell's house for about four hours eating and drinking Cola was ready to go. She had to shit real bad and she didn't want to take a shit in Cozell's momma crib so she left. Cola couldn't hold her shit no longer so she went into the alley behind a garbage can and handled her business.

Bogus Azz Hood Chick/ PattiCake Taylor 128

Realizing she didn't have no tissue after the fact Cola had to take off one of her socks to wipe her ass. Cola ass was sore and raw because her shit came out like water. Finally, Cola made it home, took her a hot bath and then called her other man Steve. She was mad at him because he wasn't coming over like he used too.

Steve had finally made it over. Cola popped some popcorn and made some cherry kool-aid so they could have a cuddle movie night but instead Steve wanted to fuck. Steve tore that pussy up for about an hour then jumped up and said he had to go.

Steve went into the bathroom to take a shower. Cola was beyond pissed, she went through his pants pockets got his cell phone and got his baby momma number out his phone. Right before he came out the shower Cola sprayed the inside of his boxers with glitter and his T-shirt as well, she wanted to make sure his baby momma knew he was fucking somebody else. Steve thought he was Mr. Playa and thought…

Bogus Azz Hood Chick/ PattiCake Taylor

Cola didn't know he was staying with his baby momma but tonight would be the night he would find out that his game was weak as fuck.

After 30 minutes Cola called Steve's phone, when he didn't answer Cola called Londea his baby momma. "Hello" a female voice said, "is this Londea" Cola asked with a smart mouth. "Yes" Londea said and "who the hell is this"? "Ummmm this Cola is Steve there"? "Why" Londea asked, "who want to know about my man". "Me", Cola responded, "your so called man fucking me, that is all". "Bitch please" Londea screamed "my man ain't fucking you". "Bitch please my ass" Cola screamed back.

"Tell that nigga to strip". "What"? Londea asked. "You a slow bitch" Cola screamed through the phone. "I tell you what act like you about to give him some head or something, I promise you, you will find a rude awaking". "Bitch, what you mean" Londea spit. "Bitch" "I mean check that nigga boxers and you will find glitter all up in his shit".

Bogus Azz Hood Chick/ PattiCake Taylor 130

"I sprayed his boxers and T-shirt while he was in my shower, he's a dumb ass nigga". "Now when you see the shit, see how he will explain he ain't fucking , BAM with a Boom Kack"!!

"Matter of fact, tell me how he will explain he ain't fucking Cola Krown Blue Royalty". CLICK! Cola hung up.

Londea and Cola had words before, but this time she had to make it known to check the dick and not the bitch. Londea started in on Steve asking him fifty questions and of course he was lying and denying everything. Steve was telling Londea that Cola was lying and that she just trying to break up a happy home. "I ain't seen that hoe in months" he said. When Steve said that, Londea decided that she would take Cola's advice and do a little role play with Steve so she could see if indeed there were glitter in his boxers.

Londea began to kiss Steve, he loosen up as the passionate tongue mixture of his woman touch his. Londea turned out the lights and unbutton Steve's pants. He was excited because she had never gone that far before…

Bogus Azz Hood Chick/ PattiCake Taylor

he was thinking he was about to get what he been waiting for. He had been asking Londea to suck his dick for the longest.

As soon as Steve came out his boxers Londea flicked the lights on and to both of their surprise there was sliver glitter everywhere.

Londea broke down and cried, after all Steve had still been fucking Cola. Londea put Steve out.

Cola and Steve fucked every so often, he just made sure to take all his clothes to the bathroom with him when they were finished.

Cola was sitting at home waiting on Cozell to call. Cozell ended up back in jail after getting into it with some nigga on the block and cutting off his house arrest band. Cozell had been calling Chops collect. Chops was a nick named he started calling Cola after the pork chop conversation and all the lip gloss print she would leave on his dick after sex. Cola was holding her man down. She was doing what was needed to be done, after all he was holding her down a little bit…

while he was out.

Cola visited sent him money, the whole nine yards. When Corzell paroled out Cola was happy but things quickly changed when he left Cola high and dry.

Cozell heard Cola was wild and fucking every nigga in site, to make Cola angry Cozell went and got him a high yellow albino looking woman. He knew Cola didn't take kindly to light skinned women and indeed Cola was heated because everybody knew this would piss her the fuck off. It was all good in Cola's book, she had several men including Steve he liked the drama that's why he stayed around.

Steve just dropped Cola off a few hundred dollars so she could go to Ever Black. Ever Black was a big mall that the locals nicknamed because of the over flow of black people that shopped there. You would have thought it was a who looked the hottest contest because everybody was dressed to kill. Cola picked up a few items at the mall and headed back home. she had to do a double take as she exited the train at 95th and the

Bogus Azz Hood Chick/ PattiCake Taylor 133

Dan Ryan.

She saw this chick that looked so familiar, as Cola got closer she knew it was her. It was Fee and that bitch had to die. Cola looked a little different since she had picked up a few pounds, but she was still fly. Her hair had grown back long and thick. She walked real close to Fee and asked for a cigarette, instead of Fee looking up she went right into her purse.

She never knew what was coming. Cola stepped back a few steps and then pushed Fee on to the train tracks. Cola hoped no one had seen her as she walked away.

As Cola walked around to the other side of the tracks some lady started yelling about a body being on the third track, everything happen so fast. The platform security came and asked everybody to leave the train area, Cola was happy with that thought. Cola hated the south side and she was ready to move back to the west side. She pondered on what lie she could use to move. I gotta find me a job before the State start tripping Cola said to herself. The next morning Cola headed out west.

Bogus Azz Hood Chick/ PattiCake Taylor 134

She had a plan to try and get a job at Moo & Oink as a chitterling cleaner and she did. The pay was shitty and so was the chitterlings but Cola wasn't tripping. The guy who interviewed Cola not only hired her on the spot but she knew that he would also give in to her plan.

As Cola played peek a boo during the interview by closing and opening her legs as he talked it became hard for him to focus, he was too busy looking at Cola's pussy.

He got aroused and he wanted to fuck. White men always wanted a taste of black women. No matter how they talked about blacks they wanted some black pussy. Cola saw the look in his eyes. He begin to undress Cola with his eyes, looking her up and down. Cola said with a smile "you want this don't you". The interviewer just looked and said nothing. Cola then got up and started kissing him. As soon as she did he got ruff, pulling her hair and all, Cola had to ask him to calm down. He then put his hands under her skirt, his eyes lit up when he realized Cola wasn't wearing any panties.

Bogus Azz Hood Chick/ PattiCake Taylor 135

He hurried up and pulled down his pants and started humping away from the back. "Damn, where is the dick"? Cola said. He said "it's in baby don't you feel it, don't it feel good"? "I'm cuming baby"! he said. Cola jumped up. "What you doing baby"? he asked.

Cola turned to him and said, "that will be one thousand dollars if you want to nut". "What the fuck, one thousand dollars he yelled, get the fuck out my office". "Oh you want me out your office" Cola yelled back at him. "How about I scream rape muther fucker". "Here bitch" as he dug in his wallet, "take this one thousand dollars and you're fired". Cola grabbed the money and told him that she would be back next week for another one thousand dollars and the week after that, and that she was keeping her damn job. Cola started laughing as nut ran down his leg. Cola went over to him and used her hand to wipe the nut that was running down his leg and then wipe it between her legs. She walked to the door and said "I'm on my way to the doctor and if your ass don't pay me your ass will be grass" then she left.

Cola was geeked that she had that one thousand dollars. She went and bought herself a Geo. Cola had seen the Geo parked on the side of the road with a "for sale" on it. It was small ass hell but it only cost eight hundred dollars and Cola was glad to have some kind of transportation.

Two weeks later… Cola moved back out west. Her new caseworker was cool, Ms. Watts was her name. Cola chuckled to herself, they were always changing caseworkers. The state let Cola move because she told them that she didn't want to have to travel back and forward on the bus to work. Cola had found her an apartment on Lotus and Monroe but she hated it now. There were just too many nigga's hanging out on the block all of a sudden.

Cola was getting in her car when some dude stepped to her trying to get his mack on. "Is this the price you gotta pay for being cute, geesh, every time I turn around some dust bucket is in my face" Cola mumble. "What's up Cutie, were your man at"? the ugly dude asked Cola?

Cola turned around from her car and asked "where's your damn woman"? He said "I ain't got one unless you want to be her". Cola laughed and said "I don't fuck with broke nigga's". "I ain't broke" he said as he pull out a stack of money that looked like all dollar bills.

"What's your name baby girl"?, Cola looked and said "Neverland". This dumb ass nigga responded by saying "Neverland is a pretty name for a pretty lady". "So Neverland when can a nigga take you out"? dude asked. Cola couldn't do nothing but laugh, "Never nigga because you will never land this". "I know all you see is fresh meat but I don't fuck with lame ass nigga on the block". Cola turned around to get in her car when she heard him say "fat bitch".

Cola was hurt by that comment, she had gained 40lbs but she thought she was thicker than a snicker not fat.

Ms. Watts came by to do her monthly check in. After they were done talking and going over paperwork Ms. Watts informed Cola that there was another girl on independent living that lived next door named LaDonna.

"Oh ok that's what's up" Cola said. After Ms. Watts left Cola went next door to introduce herself to LaDonna. "Omg gat damn it"... Cola thought laughing to herself.

LaDonna was ugly dot com, she was balded headed and needed a few tracks. One thing she did have was a killer body as if the gym was her second home with Cola gaining weight she had something else to add to her hate list, light skinned girls, gaps in the teeth and any girl with a shape better then hers. Cola had being doing her fake slim fast diet. Slim fast and salad today and ten chicken wings with fries next week.

Cola and LaDonna became real cool. They started hanging out every day, going shopping and just kicking it with guys they meet. Cola was trying to get another house phone she was tired of having to go to LaDonna's crib for all her phone calls. Cola would have had a phone if Cozell would have paid her bill once he got out of prison like he promised.

Bogus Azz Hood Chick/ PattiCake Taylor

The next day Cola was in Walgreens getting her some more Slim Fast while it was on sale. While in line this dude came up and asked if she had change for hundred dollar bill.

"No" Cola said, besides she didn't know if it was a set up or not, you had to be careful because people would set you up then robbed you. "I just know", "I just know you got change for a hundred dollars Red" Cola heard the man say, "I'm sure your pockets stay fat sexy Red". Matter of fact dude said, "you can have this hundred right here". Cola turned around and saw a red bone female putting the money in her bra.

Cola busted out and said, "just because she light don't mean it right". Dude told Cola to stop hating, he pulled out another hundred to pay for his stuff he then told the cashier to add Red bone's stuff to his bill and give her the change. Cola just rolled her eyes as she paid for her Slim Fast.

"Damn" she thought, speaking of money Sam ain't been at work. Cola kept calling Moo & Oink from an outside line hoping to reach Sam, she wanted that thousand dollars.

Bogus Azz Hood Chick/ PattiCake Taylor 140

Cola was informed that he was no longer at that store. Cola wasn't slow, he probably did a store transfer. After working only a week Cola was let go for some unknown reason. Her paperwork stated she didn't clean her chitterlings in a certain time. Cola just laughed it off wondering what would her next move be.

Everything seemed to be going wrong for Cola, she had no job and then her car started to act up. It's time for a hustle Cola thought, it's time to hustle some nigga.

In the meantime Cola and LaDonna became close, so close that Cola was licking her pussy. LaDonna was cashing in her food stamps and giving Cola half of her SSI check. Cola had to do something to stay afloat. LaDonna was Cola's hustle so as long as the money came, the licking came too.

LaDonna was dumb ass hell Cola thought, she would cash her stamps in for a bitch when she had four kids to feed. It must have been her body because her face was ah mess dot com but nigga's didn't care.

Bogus Azz Hood Chick/ PattiCake Taylor 141

She was a Ug-Ussy in their eyes, she had a pussy with a ugly face.

It was getting hot outside. Cola had been on the west side four months and hadn't seen her mother Marlene so she decided to go visit. Marlene was still a little pissed that Cola didn't want to come home after she had gotten herself clean. Marlene had cooked Cola's favorite meat which was chicken.

Cola ate her chicken with mac & cheese, greens, yams and garlic bread. After 30 minutes Cola left. Cola's car broke down and since she didn't have no money to fix it, she was back on the bus. It never failed that when Cola be out and about nigga's be all in her face and today was no different.

Some fly ass nigga pulled up in a drop top trying his damnest to lay his mac down. He offered Cola a ride but she said no thinking of all the shit she had went through with nigga's and there free rides. Dude gave Cola his number, "call me anytime" he said, you got my cell, pager and home number. "Nigga you must got some money with all this going on"

Bogus Azz Hood Chick/ PattiCake Taylor 142

Cola said aloud by mistake. He just laughed and said "my name Chauntee, holla" and he drove off. A few days later Cola called Chauntee, he invited her to come over. Chauntee only lived six blocks away. Normally Cola wouldn't fuck with a nigga in the hood but what the hell, she thought. Chauntee offered to pick Cola up but she told him that it was okay because she needed the exercise, "I'm on my fake diet" she laughed.

Cola finally made it to his house, she was amazed by how his crib looked, it was sharp as hell. He told her to make herself comfortable in the living room when all the sudden Cola noticed something strange. Was this muther fucker cripple or something, his legs was bent into a knock knee position and he walked with a stomp as if one of his legs was longer then the other. "What the hell" Cola said out loud. "You said something my love" Chauntee asked, as he finished preparing the meal that he had cooked for Cola. "I just thought about something Cola said, I need to leave but I'll be back".

Bogus Azz Hood Chick/ PattiCake Taylor 143

The next day Cola did go back to see Chauntee but she made it clear to herself he would only be her money man. That's it, that's all! Things went crazy when Cola started to have feelings in the three months they had been together. Not only was Chauntee dropping money but he could fuck his ass off. He was fucking Cola so good that she cried every time. He did wonders with his mouth piece as well, had Cola on cloud ten.

"Damn" Cola said, "what you trying to do have a bitch nose open"? Chauntee laughed and said "no baby not at all with a grin". Cola got up to go and freshen up, as she was about to use the washroom she noticed a straw cut into small pieces and some open foil with white power in it.

"What the fuck" Cola said, "this nigga using drugs". "I can't get with this shit, my nose is close shut now AND when I leave his crib this time, he won't ever see me again" Cola said to herself.

A few weeks later Cola had met her a new boo named Cassarious but everybody called him Cass for short.

Bogus Azz Hood Chick/ PattiCake Taylor 144

He was on house arrest and selling drugs from the mailbox of the building he lived in. Cass asked Cola to come visit him since he couldn't come pass his gate. Cola and LaDonna caught the bus to go see him because Cola didn't want to go alone. They were outside having a good conversation until one of Cass's customers came and that's when he excuse himself for a second. Cass and the hype went into the hallaway and after that all you heard was a big pa pow boom kack.

LaDonna started running while Cola was just standing there frozen and couldn't move. When LaDonna noticed Cola wasn't behind her, she ran back and grabbed her by the arm. thirty minutes later Cola and LaDonna went back to Cass crib to see if he was cool. The paramedics were just getting there. They were hella slow when it came to black people in the hood.

Since Cola and LaDonna were there, the police also questioned them. Cola said she didn't see nothing and didn't know nothing but big mouth LaDonna started raving on about what had happen.

Bogus Azz Hood Chick/ PattiCake Taylor 145

The police asked LaDonna for her address and phone number then the bitch had the nerve to get scared. The police had started to harass Cola because LaDonna told them that she and Cola were friends who stayed in the same building and that Cass was Cola's boyfriend. Not soon after Cola asked her caseworker if she could move because of the Cass situation and LaDonna's big ass mouth.

Cola felt her life was in danger and she wasn't for sure if the shooter saw her face. The police were getting so deep like it was a murder case or something, that scared LaDonna and she was asking Cola to stay over at her place every night.

Weeks later Cola ended up moving up north, it was rainbow gay city. Most gay people lived up north because there lifestyle was accepted more there than any other part of Chicago.

Belmont was one of the main streets to be on, clubs, adult toy stores and more. Cola had moved up north just in time for gay pride weekend.

Bogus Azz Hood Chick/ PattiCake Taylor

Cola had changed a lot, she was kicking the door down at 200lbs. Cola carried her weight well but that hottie body was way out of there. Cola had become confused, she didn't know if she wanted to be a feminine woman or a studdy woman. Living up north you saw some of the hottest women the only thing was they were born male. They looked better then any real woman after paying thousands of dollars.

Cola had gone into a boyish look. Her butters were down her back, she had hazel contacts and she wore her pants with a slight sag. Cola thought she was fly and the ladies made it known that she was. She had all the ladies on her. Cola was nineteen and didn't have shit but the apartment the state had provided for her. Cola had no worries, the ladies made sure she had everything.

Cola had her little boo thang named Gia. She was so into Cola that she would let Cola drop her off at work and keep her car. While Gia was at work Cola would hook up with her other boo thang Starr. Starr wined and dined Cola and she loved it.

Bogus Azz Hood Chick/ PattiCake Taylor

Cola had it made she now consider herself to be in the "life" and now she was "family" those were some of the terms the LGBT community would use.

Co-Co is what Gia and Starr thought Cola's name was. Cola was feeling her some Gia, she was stuck on Gia's pussy. It was good and always smelled and tasted fresh.

Cola thought she was the gayest thing in the hood. She had gone and got the lesbian female symbol on her back, she got tongue pierced and a fresh fit for pride. It was Friday and pride was that Sunday. Cola decided that she wanted to go alone just in case she saw some more honey's she wanted on her team.

The next day Cola was crusing down Madison street in Gia's car when she spotted LaDonna. "hell nawl" Cola said to herself. She hadn't seen LaDonna since she moved up north.

"Hell muther fucking nawl, I know that's not LaDonna with that big ass black eye". Cola yelled from the window "LaDonna, giiiiiirl what the hell happen to your eye"? LaDonna gave Cola some bogus story about these girls jumping her and hitting her in hit in the eye with a car club.

"Oh ok" Cola said "looks like more of a fist print but ok girl, long as you know domestic violence is never cool". "You need a ride somewhere"? "No" LaDonna said I'm waiting on my ride to come.

"Aiight" Cola said and drove off. Thirty minutes later when Cola drove back pass Ladonna was still standing there. "Ride my ass" Cola said, "this bitch hooking". Cola couldn't tell at first because it was hot out and most woman dress hoochie but it was confirmed when some pimp jumped out his truck and slap LaDonna to the ground hitting her a few times before dragging her to the alley. Cola (being nosy) wanted to see what else the pimp was gonna do to LaDonna. He had her sucking his dick in broad day light. Cola drove off and headed back north, she decided she was going to stop at the Belmont Heights and see what lezbo's were out. Cola stepped out Gia's car flexing her air ones, saggy shorts and wife beater.
Women were every where and if you looked like you had

Bogus Azz Hood Chick/ PattiCake Taylor 149

money those bitches were on you like bee's on honey. "What's up C", some girl said throwing Cola out of deep thought, "You looking too good" Cola turned around and said "who the fuck you talking too"? "You Big C" that girl said. Cola said "Big C huh that sounds kinda hot", "what's your name shorty"? "That's it baby, you hit it right on the nail, my name Shorty".

Shorty was stacked, she had a little gut but it was all good. She was 4'11 about 140lbs and had a watermelon ass. Shorty was bold as hell, she went for what she wanted. She walked right up Cola and started tongue kissing her down. After that was over Shorty asked Cola if she had a woman. Cola said "yeah, she right here baby". "Big C and Shorty sounds good to me".

Cola then asked Shorty "how she knew her anyways". Shorty laughed a little and said "who don't know you baby". "I guess" Cola said laughing to herself. "Anyways I holla, I'm out, I gotta go pick up my wifey". "Your wifey" Shorty yelled.

"Yeah" Cola said "did I muther fucking stutter"? "but I

Bogus Azz Hood Chick/ PattiCake Taylor 150

thought you said I was your girl" Shorty said. "And you believed that shit"? "Bitch I don't even know your ass and if I'm so damn popular you should have known I had a girl". "But yeah Big C will holla at you soon" said Cola. Shorty look on as Cola got in the car and drove away.

It was Sunday....

Pride day had come and this would be Cola's first time going. "Damn" Cola chuckled, look at all these people in this parade. Polices, lawyers, doctors, men, woman, teens some of everybody and they momma. This shit was crazy as hell.

Cola was in a daze seeing people come outside damn near naked and even worse looking a hot mess. "Shiiit I know I'm sharp", Cola was saying out loud to no one, "my wifey Gia hit me with five hundred dollars". "She bought me some fresh J's, some nice shorts, a white on white wife beater and she got my butters was whipped". Cola began to laugh, "hmmmm.. seems like all eyes are on me". At that thought some light skinned chick came walking up to Cola...

Bogus Azz Hood Chick/ PattiCake Taylor 151

"Are you alone" she asked. "Yeah" Cola said "for a minute, I'm waiting on my peeps" she lied.

"What's your name Shorty"? Cola asked. "I'm Dimples and you"? "you can call me Krown" Cola replied.

"Well Krown, I can stand here with you until your friends come" Dimples said. "Cool, I need a little company anyways this shit new to me" Cola replied. Dimples would be just that company to Cola until she figured out her next move. Dimples name fit her because she had dimples every where but her face and this hoe had the nerve to have on white shorts with dimples all in her ass…

Cola laughed with an outburst, "everybody knows COLA can't stand light skinned bitches but today Cola a.k.a Krown was gonna used the bitch".

"You looking damn good Dimples" Cola replied. "You are too Krown, that's your name right" Dimples asked . "Yeah, ain't that what I told you" Cola snapped.

"Yeah but I thought your name was Cola" Dimples replied.

Bogus Azz Hood Chick/ PattiCake Taylor 152

"It is bitch, and how the hell you know that"? Cola yelled. "Oh my home girl told me, it's nothing major, so chill with the bitch word" Dimples replied rolling her eyes. "Whatever bitch" Cola said.

Vendors were every where selling all type of stuff so Cola decided to test her skills and see if she could get some money out of Dimples. Cola and Dimples walked and talked all up Belmont, Cola was asking for everything in sight and Dimples was buying it all.

Cola thought herself "why I gotta spend the few dollars that I have left over when I dropped Gia off at work she hit me with a couple extra dollars". "If this yellow bitch wants to spend all her money, I will make sure she spends it all on me". When Dimples ran out of cash from spending all her money on Cola they headed to a ATM to get more. Cola thought she better show Dimples a little more attention so she can get them few extra dollars.

Cola began to kiss Dimples as if she was the last woman on

earth.

Dimples smelled so good though, that was until Cola reached down and played with her little coochie through her shorts. Cola got want she deserved, a hand full of tuna. Bitch smelled like bath and body up top but that coochie was another story.

How nasty was it for Dimples to let someone she didn't even know play with her pussy and outside at that. Cola was completely turned off as (if she wasn't already).

Cola told Dimples she would be back, Cola lied and said she needed to find a restroom. Cola disappeared in the crowd while walking down Belmont. She spotted a few people from the hood she knew so she decided to chill with them for a minute.

Cola turned around to her right and yelled "hell nawl, I know that's not who I think it is". "Ain't this a bitch, when I asked this hoe was she coming to pride she told me no". Gia was standing their all in some bitch face.

Bogus Azz Hood Chick/ PattiCake Taylor

They had the nerve to have on matching outfits. Cola walked over a few steps and as Gia and the other bitch kissed Cola pulled Gia by the back of her shirt. "Gia, what the fuck you doing here with Starr"? "You thought you was a player muther fucker"! Gia spat, "who the fuck are you to play me Gia continued you ain't shit and you ain't got shit, since you fucking us both we might as well be together". "Bitch I thought your ass had to work, lying ass hoe" Cola yelled at Gia. "Who the fuck you calling a bitch and a hoe Co-Co" Gia yelled back? "You a bitch, a confused bitch at that", Gia spat back with attitude.

Cola slapped Gia so hard that tears fell from face. Cola was pissed like a muther fucker. "Bitch just watch, you think this little stunt is cute and funny, I guarantee that I will have the last laugh Cola said as she walked off heated". "Dumb ass bitch" Cola said fussing to herself, "stupid bitch don't know me, don't know where I lived, hell I was always at her house after I picked her dumb ass up from work".

Bogus Azz Hood Chick/ PattiCake Taylor 155

"Bitch don't even know my real name". Cola kept talking to herself as she walked off "and bitch I'm driving your car now bitch haha who laughing now bitch". "Stupid hoe you forgot I got keys to your crib too". "I'm gonna steal all I can and yeah bitch while you out having fun you won't know what hit your ass and I'm going to burn your car"." Haha, haha, haha bitch who laughing now".

It was 3am and Gia and Starr had a great time without a care in the world. "Baby we had fun tonight at the after set" Starr said to Gia. "Yes we did baby, it was awesome and I'm glad I was with you" Gia said with a smile.

Starr pulled up in front of Gia's apartment, still excited about the time they had at the parade, the beach and the club. "It was the bomb" Starr said with a smile. "You wanna come upstairs with me" Gia asked Starr hoping she could get some early morning sex. "I need to call Co-Co anyways to get my car and my other set of house keys". "Yeah I'll go up Starr said, I'm still a little tipsy anyways".

Bogus Azz Hood Chick/ PattiCake Taylor

Gia fondled through her purse to find her house keys. She entered her apartment and turned the lights on, Just then Gia almost had a heart attack, "what the fuck" Gia screamed so loud, "what the fuck oh my gosh".

As she entered every room most of her stuff was gone and the rest was broken up. "I can't breathe" Starr, "I need my asthma pump". "Who the "fuck", who the fuck did this". I gotta call the police. Riiiiiing…. "911 what's your emergency"? "Yes ummmm somebody broke into my apartment, oh hell nawl, no wait a minute".

"Co-Co, this bitch Co-Co stole my shit". "And how do you know this" the 911 operator said. "Because when I opened my door there was no forced entry". "Where does this Co-Co person live, What's her first and last name"? "When was the last time you saw her"? the operator asked. "Huh"! Gia had a dumb look on her face. "I, I don't even know, how dumb of me, she was always at my house and Co-Co was the name she gave me, we were just cool…

Bogus Azz Hood Chick/ PattiCake Taylor 157

I didn't think things were gonna be this way".

"She seemed so down to earth and nice". "Wait"! Gia screamed "she has my car too, oh my god". "What kind of car do you have and what's your plate number" the operator asked in shock herself. "It's a 94'Caviler the new one, I just got it six months ago" Gia said through tears.

"It's Purple and my plates say (A HOT GIA 1)". "Hold on ma'am" the police operator said to Gia. "Ma'am are you there"? "Yes" Gia said. "We have a report of a 94 Caviler that was set on fire on the west side of Chicago, you will need to go to your local police department and file a report". "Okay thank you" Gia said, pissed at her damn self.

Starr and Gia headed to the police station to make a report on Co-Co about her crib and car. Since Gia didn't have enough information on Cola the police said it wasn't much they could do. But they would keep the information she provided on file. Gia cried all the way back home, Starr did her best to try and comfort her. Gia was so upset at what happened that she told

Starr that she was no longer going to mess with woman.

She also told Starr that she didn't want to be with her. "I'm sorry", Gia said to Starr as she exited her car before going into the crib. Little did Gia know, Cola was waiting for her in the dark. Cola had been there all that time in the closet when Gia first came home but she had Starr with her so Cola had to put her plans on hold. Cola was gonna make sure Gia pay for her actions.

Gia laid in her bed which was now on the floor and she cried and cried, she didn't even hear Cola come up behind her. As Cola beat Gia with a bat Gia just laid there taking it. Gia didn't scream or anything. A few moments later Gia was dead. Cola left Gia's crib as nothing had ever happened. No one knew her like that in the area so she knew she was all good, she didn't have to hide out. Cola made a mental note that she would have to kill Starr next because if she put two and two together she would probably go to the police. "If Starr knew what was good for her, she would keep her muther fucking mouth closed and get the message through the death of Gia" Cola mumble!

Over the next few months Cola was going to all the hottest gay clubs in Chicago and being a player, it was Cola's persona that made all the ladies want her, they fell in love and gave up all there money. Cola met this girl named Romance. Cola was feeling her real hard. Romance must have had a powerful tool because Cola went and found her a job and was spending all her check on Romance.

After six months of dating Cola felt like things were changing between them. The sex had become different and Romance hadn't been acting herself. Cola had heard that Romance's baby daddy had gotten out of prison and she didn't want to tell Cola because he was very controlling.

One evening Cola just popped up at Romance's house and Romance's baby daddy opened the door with a frown. He started yelling at Cola to leave. Cola refused saying Romance was her woman and she wasn't leaving. Cola must have forgotten she was a woman and not a man, dude hauled off and

Bogus Azz Hood Chick/ PattiCake Taylor 160

knocked her off the porch to the ground and stomped the shit out of her.

Luckily for Cola the police rolled up on him before he could finish that beat down. Cola pressed charges on him and sent him back on his merry way to prison. Romance gave Cola a nasty look and the middle finger as she watched from the window. Cola said to Romance as she yelled at the window, "don't trip, to watch her muther fucking front because she'll be back in due time".

It was a cold chilly night in Chicago and Cola could never understand why the neighborhood boys would stand outside and freeze just to make a few dollars when they could have gotten a Mcdonald's job. "I guess people have to do what they need to do to survive" Cola mumbled as she walked slowly from the pain to get in the house.

It had been two months since Romance's baby daddy had jumped on Cola. She had started losing a lot of weight because she had to eat her food through a straw. Cola could only have liquids such as soup, because he had broken her jaw in the mist of the beat down.

Once Cola healed, she decided she would get a membership at a health club so she could get toned and sexy for her birthday. Cola would be the big 2 0 and when she turned 21 the system would let her go. Cola needed to go to school or find a great job of some sort before it was too late because once the system discharge you it was a done deal.

A few months later… Cola was at her old weight and had a body to die for. It must have been the way she walked, she seemed to have every man's nose open at the gym every time she came to work out. Cola had always been cute but since she had lost all that extra weight she noticed she was getting more attention and she was loving it. She had to laugh at the situation. "hmmmm" she laughed to herself, "I guess the saying is true, if you were small or even had a body nigga's would be flocking to you".

Cola seemed to have done an 360 because one day she woke

Bogus Azz Hood Chick/ PattiCake Taylor 162

up and felt good about herself.

She felt like an new person inside and she wanted a new start on life.

Cola's mind told her to go to church, something she had never done before. As Cola sat there listening to the preacher it was as if he was talking to her as he preached about homosexuality being a sin. Cola kept turning her head around and around trying to figure out who Pastor Monroe was talking too or about. As he ended he asked if anyone wanted to say a few words, Cola stood and she waited for her turn.

"Praise the lord everybody, my name is Cola Krown ummmm, just call me Cola. I done came a mighty long way, I'm so happy to be here today. God has blessed me and I feel it's time for me to get my shit together, Oops I'm sorry". "It's time for me to make a change in my life. So Pastor, saint's and aint's, if you a true believer in god please pray for me Thank you".

After service something happened to Cola she never thought

would happen, she had an attraction to men again.

One of the finest men came walking up to Cola, she started to sweat little rain drops from her forehead. His name was doctor feel good to Cola but she heard someone call him Yohance. He was so sexy as he walked with his red and black tailored suit on. Cola was digging his look.

"Hey sister how you doing"? Yohance said to her. "Hello" Cola replied. "Would you like to go down stairs and join me for Sunday dinner my treat"? Yohance asked. Cola smiled and said "yes I would". Yohance's teeth were super white as he smiled, he was chocolate, had a bald head and was slightly bow-legged, he had to be at least 6feet. They ate Sunday dinner as they had small talk. All the woman in church was looking at Cola sideways.

Cola laughed to herself as she flirted with Yohance during their meal. When they were done Yohance offered to take Cola home, and of course she took him up on his offer since he was a man of God.

Bogus Azz Hood Chick/ PattiCake Taylor 164

How could she say no to a fine looking church brother like Yohance. He finally pulled up in front of Cola's home they exchanged numbers and he told her he would call her when he got home.

Yohance walked Cola to the door and gave her a soft kiss on her cheek. "Thank God I got a home phone" Cola screamed as she ran up her stairs, "well Thank You Sharissa for letting me use one of your twelve kids social security numbers". "Fifty dollars wasn't a bad deal" Cola mumbled and laughed to herself, "who does shit like that, nobody but dust bucket hypes".

"Oh shit forgive me lord, my bad, work on my tongue lord in Jesus name". Cola sat on the living room floor right by the phone and turned on her T.V, hoping that Yohance would indeed call.

After that beat down over a bitch Cola asked herself was it even worth being with a woman. God had saved her life so in return Cola would try and do right by God. It may be hard she thought but having a God fearing man in my life, might be just what I need.

As Cola was in deep thought, Yohance called. Cola was all smiles as she heard that deep Barry White sounding voice of her new man. Cola's smile quickly turn into a frown when she found out Yohance wasn't a man of god. He only came to church because he was looking for a nigga named Derrance. It was payback time for Derrance and word on the street was that Derrance had gotten out the drug game and gotten saved.

After an all niter on the phone Cola wanted her some Yohance. He was a bad boy to the fullest, he had his own money and was now running Daddy B's old spot after he took out Melo. He was the new nigga in charge. Crazy thing was Cola wondered how long Yohance would be around before someone took him out, seemed to be a cycle of killing to get to the top.

For the first time in months Cola was able to eat normally. She could eat whatever she wanted. She still ate real slow because she was scared that she was going break her jaw again. Cola wanted some fried chicken so she headed to Popeyes chicken and got a ten piece chicken special with red beans and rice, mashed potatoes and five biscuits. She couldn't wait to get home to smash her food. Cola ate all that then headed for McDonald's she wasn't hungry but she wanted it just because she was able to eat it. Once Cola got to McDonald's she was pissed that the line wasn't moving due to some girls lip boxing over some dude. As Cola turned to leave she heard a scream, she turned around to see the girl was pulling the McDonald's crew member from behind the counter giving her all the business with her fist.

Finally after twenty minutes or so somebody broke up the fight. "That's the dumbest thing ever" Cola said out loud, but meant to say it to herself instead "but oh well yep, I said it out loud, you a dumb bitch". "Female's be blowing me when they attack the other woman, what about that no good cheating ass man". The girl gave Cola a look. Cola stepped out her 5inch heels, pulled down her pants, held her ass wide open and asked the girl what was up? "You can kiss this big ole ass" Cola said, "Bitch you don't want none of this". The girl rushed at Cola to receive a fist to the mouth getting a tooth knock out. Pa pow bitch with a boom kack!

   Later on that night Cola tried calling Yohance but for some reason the lady on the other end kept saying she had the wrong number. "Are you sure" Cola spoke into the phone, "I'm looking at the number right here 555-5456, let me just hang up and call this number again". The lady picked up the phone with an attitude, "didn't I tell your ass you had the wrong number the lady screamed into the phone". "There's nobody here by that name just me and my husband Yusef, there's no fucking Yohance here". "Oh god" Cola said, "please tell me, I'm not about to go through this bullshit again with nigga's lying about their names". "You see I meet this fine brother at church Sunday and this the number he gave me when we switch number's" Cola talked into the phone. "What does he look like the woman asked"?

"Oh wow" Cola said "he's tall, sexy, and chocolate with a bald head, kinda bow-legged". The lady screamed and then said "can you repeat that". Cola repeated what she had said and indeed it was the woman husband. He had given Cola the right number but the wrong name not knowing that his wife would be back so soon from out of town. She had gone to take care of her sick mother.

Cola really didn't believe her because she heard someone in church call him Yohance, maybe she was tripping. Twanika, Yusef's wife couldn't believe her ears, while she was away her no good husband was out cheating.

"Wait a second" Cola said, "I haven't slept with Yohance yet so if this is your husband, he hasn't cheated with me". Twanika invited Cola over because she wanted to make sure this wasn't her husband. Cola told Twanika she didn't have a car. "That's fine girly, I have an car" Twanika said a little too

Bogus Azz Hood Chick/ PattiCake Taylor 169

loud I'll come to you. Twanika asked for Cola's address, grabbed her wedding photo album and headed to Cola's place.

"I hope this bitch don't start shit, I don't feel like fighting today". Cola said to herself "be nice". "What the fuck, that's Yohance", Cola said to herself, "lying muther fucker". Cola didn't want to be the cause of a unhappy home, so she lied to Twanika, she made a mental note to herself to cuss Yohance ass out. Twanika was satisfied with Cola answer. Twanika invited Cola over for dinner for the misunderstanding. Cola accepted dying to see this nigga reaction as she sat at their dinner table. Sure enough Yohance had the shit face, when he walked into the kitchen seeing Cola smacking on garlic bread.

Yohance asked his wife, who was her new friend. Cola begin to laugh loudly as Twanika explained the story. Yohance had a huge smile on his face until Cola passed him a note saying she wanted ten thousand dollars for lying to his wife.

After dinner, movie and wine Yohance told Cola he wanted one on one time with his wife. Twanika smiled, Cola rubbed

Bogus Azz Hood Chick/ PattiCake Taylor

her fingers together in a gesture she wanted her cash.

Yohance walked Cola to the door and told her he wasn't giving her one red cent. Later that night Cola came back after an hour long bus ride. She broke into Yohance and Twanika's home, turned on the eyes on the stove and blew out the fire so the gas smell could roam the house. Thirty minutes later Cola set their kitchen on fire.

The next day Cola's caseworker just so happened to pop up to do a surprise visit. D C F S sent Cola a letter and explained she needed to go to school or find a job before they discharged her early from the program. Cola was pissed and snapped at the caseworker. "okay, damn, I'll find something are you happy now, y'all muther fucker blowing me" Cola said in anger.

Later that night Cola was watching after hours B E T video's after seeing one too many ass shakes on T.V Cola decided to try being a stripper again. "Quick cash and why not I got my body back" she smiled. There was a new owner at The Pole in the Wall named Honey Melt. He was too a stripper but only danced for the male's that was on the down low.

There was a private room for them when they wanted to excuse themselves from their woman or home boys and see him.

Cola asked if she could come in for an interview after she got that nasty thought out her head of Honey Melt popping his penis in the back room, nigga's were supposed to go to The Pole in the Wall for pussy not dick.

Honey Melt said she could come in but he wanted to know what she looked like. Well Cola spoke into the phone, "I am a dollar piece, I'm 5'4, 145lbs thick in all the right places". "I got ass for days, long hair down my back all mines, no weave in my shit, oh my bad, but I had to keep it real". "I got mad sex appeal, you will see tomorrow". "Bye" Cola said and she hung up.

The next day Cola was a little salty that it was kinda cool out and that she had to get on the bus and go all the way to the south side to The Pole in the Wall. When Cola arrived to the club it was different…

Honey Melt had remodel and changed the name to 50 shades of Honey's! Any type of women the fellas wanted. Honey Melt had at 50 shades of Honey's.

"one, two, three let's do this" Cola blew out her mouth. "Hello, my name is Cola and I'm looking for Honey" Cola said nicely to the receptionist. "Hold on a second she said, let me page him for you". "What's up Cola" a male voice said? Cola turned around and damn near gagged to death when she saw Yohance or Yusef, whatever his name was standing before her. "Calm down Cola" he said, "look like you seen a damn ghost or something".

Cola just looked and looked again as her heart beat faster then any race car, she turned around and started walking towards the door. Yohance grabbed Cola's arm. Cola yanked her arm and screamed loudly. "I can't work for you what type of games you playing nigga"? Yohance laughed "oh nawl this not my shit, this my home boy shit". "Whatever nigga I don't want to be no where near you or your crazy wife".

"That bitch came to my house". Yohance eyes got big "and yeah Yusef why the fuck you give me your number and you knew you was married".

"Cola your ass is crazy as hell, I ain't married and Yusef is my twin brother, that bitch was my sister in law". "what the hell you mean was"? Cola asked? "My brother's crib caught fire some type of way, it burned so quickly that they couldn't get out". "They stayed in the burning house trying to save their kids". Cola's eyes got big this time! "Their kids" she asked. "Yeah Yohance said, they had two sets of twins Two and Three years old". Cola began to cry. Yohance tried to comfort her, "don't cry" he said, "I'm gonna kill the nigga that did that shit". Cola perked up quickly, "how you know it was a nigga" she asked? "That bitch ass sister in law of mine was cheating on my brother". "My family and I found out that those twins was not my brothers through DNA". "Oh how sad" Cola said and then turned back to the receptionist and asked where Honey was.

Bogus Azz Hood Chick/ PattiCake Taylor 174

"He'll be right with you just have a seat the receptionist said". "Well can I use your ladies room while I wait" Cola asked. "Yeah it's in the back". Cola scrolled on to the back being nosy as hell, she started opening doors to see what was happening. "Ugh, "o.m.g" Honey Melt was sucking some nigga dick, that shit nasty as hell". "Guess I'm double standard" Cola laughed to herself, but to her that was nasty, two nigga's fucking. In another room some girls were getting high and in the room next door to that one there was a threesome going on with two dudes and one female. Just when Cola was saying to herself maybe I don't want to work here, someone ask her could they help her. Cola jump and gagged when she saw some ugly, bumpy faced dude standing before her. "Oh I'm sorry" she said, "I'm looking for the ladies room". "I'll show you he said and then I'll be ready to interview you". "By the way I'm Honey".

Cola did a double take, "you look nothing like your picture" she said, Cola laughed so hard that she damn near pissed on herself wondering did he go gargle after sucking that man dick in the other room she peeped in.

That same night Cola got hired and showed out on that pole. she went by the named Ms. P.A.T "Pussy, Ass & Titties" and she made two thousand dollars in one night. Nigga's loved new pussy. "This what I'm talking about" Cola said out loud as she changed her clothes to go home. Climax another stripper asked Cola if she needed a lift home? "Thanks but no thanks" Cola said to her.

Climax was one of the ladies in the back room getting high and Cola refused to become a dope head. "Ain't no birds flocking together on this end" Cola mumbled. I don't knock nobody for what they do Cola thought to herself "but I refuse to be a head nodding hype in the streets and have everybody shaking they damn head at me".

Cola was getting it in at 50 shades of Honey's every night. There was this one dude that came to the club every night to watch P.A.T "Pussy Ass & Titties" but every time Cola would ask him for a one on one he would say no. "He must be here to see Honey Melt" Cola laughed to herself.

"I should ask him but with a name like Body Bag I'll pass" Cola thought as she kept it moving. Word on the street was that Body Bag would kill a muther fucker at anytime and at any place and wouldn't give two fucks.

That same night all hell broke loose in the club. Nobody knew what was going on but somebody came in and knew what they wanted and it was that nigga Body Bags. One of the dudes that entered the club poured gasoline on Body Bag and set him on fire as everybody tried to break for the door.

Body Bag lived but he had a new name, people can be so cruel. They started calling him Crispy. He still came to the club after Honey Melt re-opened from the damages. Now Crispy started to request Ms. P.A.T "Pussy Ass & Titties" for one on one, as bad as he looked Cola didn't turn down that cash. She just laughed at his crispy burnt ass.

Everything was all good at the club, Cola was making money and she had different nigga's flocking to her every night trying

Bogus Azz Hood Chick/ PattiCake Taylor 177

to smell her Pussy, Ass, and Titties.

Some kind of way Climax found her way into Cola's life. It started as small talk when Climax came to work with a black eye, she told Cola that her son's father beat her up for not giving him money to get high with. Through her sobs Climax stressed how she had her own addiction and six kids by six different men, she was taking care of her kids on her own because their dad's didn't provide.

Climax founded comfort in Cola. She loved the fact Cola never judged her. She needed a friend and Cola was a good friend to her. Many of nights Climax would curl up like as a baby would do and cry through her swollen eyes. Cola expressed time after time how domestic violence was never okay and she needed to find strength to leave her youngest son's father.

Cola only wanted to be friends with Climax, but Climax stressed how she wanted to be more then friends, she told Cola that she would leave her son's father if they could be together.

Bogus Azz Hood Chick/ PattiCake Taylor 178

Cola tried to explain how she was no longer into women, she went to church and the preacher preach about sin and same sex relationships was one of them.

Cola was trying her hardest to fight the feelings. As Cola was going on and on Climax got up and kissed her, before Climax knew what had happen she was on the floor from a powerful slap Cola landed on her face. "Bitch"!! "Didn't you hear what I was just saying"? "Don't ever disrespect me like that". "I'm sorry" Climax cried, "I just wanted somebody to love me". "Well you need to love your damn self first before anybody else can love you" Cola screamed at Climax. "I'm sorry for hitting you Climax, it was just a reaction" Cola said. Cola continue:

"I want somebody to care for me and love me too, but woman on woman ain't right. "Besides you be putting that shit up your nose, do you really think I want a bitch that's getting high". "Do you want the state to come take your damn kids, you getting high, your son's father getting high, he beating you, that shit ain't safe for you or your children"…

Bogus Azz Hood Chick/ PattiCake Taylor

"The state ain't no punk, they don't give two fucks about taking your kids and getting millions each year to house them".

"The state gives these foster parents pennies and most of them don't give a shit about the kids, they just want them checks". Nobody and I mean nobody will love your kids the way you love them Climax" said Cola. "How the fuck you know so much about the state" Climax said loudly.

"I know", Cola said through her own tears now. "I'm a ward of the state now, I been in five foster homes, a group home, in the nut house, now I'm on independent living housing and when I turn twenty one the system going to drop me like hot cakes". "That's why I'm dancing, trying to stack some cash before I'm discharged from the state, that's how the fuck I know". "Hell my momma couldn't get me back for years and when she had the chance I was eighteen and I didn't want to go home then". "So you need to get your shit together Nina" Cola said all in one breathe . "I need help" Climax yelled "and don't call me Nina"! "Whatever Nina, I'll do my best to help you".

Bogus Azz Hood Chick/ PattiCake Taylor

said Cola.

As Climax laid there on the floor Cola laid right by her side and said to her, "I'll be your friend and I'll love you as a friend and a sister and help you through your tough times, right now I'm going to hold you tight through your struggle and cry with you until you heal" Cola said, "Thank you" Climax said through tears. They laid there and nothing else was said for the rest of the night. Cola just held Climax all night until she was finally asleep.

Cola did something that took her by surprise she began to pray. "Father I lift my hands to you, asking you to heal and restore my friend Nina, I know without a doubt you can and you are able to help the sick". Give her the strength to find a way to live a healthy lifestyle, help her remove her and her children out of harm's way". "In Jesus name I pray". "Amen"

A week later Climax went into rehab, and Ms. Annie Climax's mom took in all her children so they wouldn't be put into a foster care. Cola was there as a support system to help

Bogus Azz Hood Chick/ PattiCake Taylor 181

Climax through. Cola even stopped dancing, and she no longer had to lie to her caseworker about working at a fast food joint. Cola explained to her caseworker she had a dying friend that needed 24/7 care because Climax's mom was older and needed help taking care of the children and she would give her a few dollars for helping out.

The caseworker stood firm when she warned Cola to find a job or else. Cola began to laugh, "I don't take well to threats"! "You got four weeks to find another job or go to school or you will be stripped from the program" Cola's Caseworker said. "Whatever" Cola replied back, "I only got one more year anyways".

Twelve weeks had past and Climax was doing very well, so well that the doctor informed her she could go home if she felt she was strong enough. Climax was trying to go home as quickly as possible, her children were split up with other relatives because her mother had passed away in her sleep. Cola told Climax how her mother was sent away like a Sunday

Bogus Azz Hood Chick/ PattiCake Taylor 182

church service, the choir was marching down the aisles singing, stomping and getting there praise on.

Cola entered the house where she stayed with her mom Marlene after the system released her for not applying herself as they called it. She asked Marlene if she could come live with her for a little while. Well of course that was like music to Marlene's ears to have her daughter home. Cola picked up the house phone to call Climax once again she had to deliver some more bad news, well to Cola it was good news.

"Nina, I'm sorry to tell you but June Bug over dosed and died" Cola tried to sound as pleasant as possible, but she was happy June Bug was out of Nina life forever. Nina sniffed a few times then replied "June Bug can't beat me no more"

A couple of months had past and Climax was doing better then ever. She was released from rehab with a pocket full of money. She bought herself a home in the suburbs, got herself a new car and had all her six kids. Ms. Annie had left Climax a nice amount of money and Climax made a promise that when she came home she was gonna look out for her friend Cola because she was there when no one else was. Cola was in a day dream as Climax pulled up to Marlene's porch.

Cola seemed to be nodding as if she was high off drugs herself. Climax rushed out her car to see what was going on. "This is fucked up Cola noooooooooooooo"! Cola was indeed higher then a kite. Climax started shaking and yelling at Cola asking her what the hell she was high off of.

"I ain't high" Cola yelled. "All I had was some weed my momma man mixed some white powder stuff with it". "Girl, he lace your weed, what the fuck" Climax screamed!

"OMG, what we gonna do Cola"? "I don't know Cola said but I want some more".

Cola had gotten hook on heroin just that fast. Jose, Marlene's boyfriend was jealous of Cola and Marlene relationship since Cola had moved in. Jose was pissed that Cola was getting more attention than him so he formulated a plan to get her kicked out by making her a dope head. Jose wanted to continue to do the things he would normally do which was shit, he slept all day and was up all night getting high and drinking all night with his ugly ass friends.

Cola had started stealing from Marlene so she could get high, she had no money and she was waiting for Climax to give her whatever money she was going give her so she could get high in peace and not have to steal.

Climax had money for Cola but now she had changed her mind about giving it to her. Climax didn't want to give Cola the fifty thousand dollars she had for her because she already knew that if she did it would have been used for drugs. Climax had been there and done that and she wanted to help Cola not destroy her.

Funny how things change when you look down or laugh at people because it was now Cola in the alley sucking dick to get her a high just like her old friend Ladonna had been doing.

In just those few weeks Cola's looks had started to change, those drugs were doing a number on her.

Bogus Azz Hood Chick/ PattiCake Taylor 185

Marlene told Cola she had to move because she wasn't gonna support no drug habit and she was tired of Cola stealing from her. Cola was piss off, "oh you will support your man drug habit huh" Cola mumble.

Cola cried out that, the last few times she didn't steal. It was Jose that stole Marlene's work check and was blaming it on Cola. He was saying that he had missing money too.

Cola was pissed and when she was done packing her bags she walked out Marlene's house with tears in her eyes and she vowed that she was gonna get Jose ass one way or another.

Cola stopped at a nearby pay phone and called her friend Climax and explained what had happened with her mom and boyfriend. Climax was in her own little world without a care in the world. She was living the life of the rich and famous and didn't even care what Cola was going through. Climax gave Cola five hundred dollars and told her to get a hotel room, she told Cola that she couldn't come stay with her.

Cola was hurt, "Bitch" she screamed "how quickly your ass

forgot, I guess you know who your friends are when you really down and out". "It's a shame Climax, a damn shame that you would treat me this way but it's cool, you live and you learn". Cola started to give Climax I was there for you speech… but she didn't, she had been there as a friend and sister and everything she did she did it from her heart.

Cola took that five hundred dollars and headed for the green line el. She went to a motel almost in the heart of downtown, she was on Roosevelt and Michigan ave.

After Cola got settled she went to a local drug store and stole her some makeup so she could cover the scares up in her face. Cola looked rough, she didn't have that pretty glow she once had. Cola was still a little heated at Climax, she decided to just let Climax be and just get over how she had been treated. "Black people get money and changes anyways" Cola mumble.

Cola was on the corner nodding her ass off, when this slick cat by the name of Day~Light, began to tell Cola sweet nothings about how he could make her life easier and

Bogus Azz Hood Chick/ PattiCake Taylor

all he wanted was seventy percent. Right then Cola knew he was a pimp. Day~Light had a sharp Cadillac and he was sharp too, outside in ninety degree weather with a five piece suit on.

Cola said no thank you to Day~Light and that seemed to have pissed him off. For some reason pimps hated rejection. Day~Light beat Cola up with no care in the world. When the ambulance arrived Cola was unconscious. Day~Light really fucked Cola up, he didn't care she was ninety eight pounds soaking wet now.

Cola had lost a lot of weight messing with that shit. She fell into a coma while she was in the hospital.

Marlene started to feel bad that she had put her child out over a man. "Dick good" Marlene said to herself, "but damn it ain't that good to choose a man over my child".

Marlene headed to hospital to check on Cola. Marlene finally made it to the hospital, she was as loud as ever saying she needed the room number for Cola Krown Blue Royalty Johnson. People turned around as they giggled a little bit.

Bogus Azz Hood Chick/ PattiCake Taylor

Marlene walked into Cola's room, then she walked out and looked at the room number again.

1024 "I got the right room" she said. She walked over to Cola's bed then began to scream and yell, "that's not my fucking daughter".

Cola didn't look like herself at all. The street life will have you looking that way, rough and down and out.

The doctor informed Marlene that Cola had a slim chance of making it and that she should call all her family together and have a talk with them. Marlene was torn up inside as she look at her only child laid up on her death bed at twenty years old, fighting for her life. Marlene went home and did something she never thought she would ever do again, she called Cola's father Slim. Slim is what everybody call him because he was tall and skinny as hell.

After calling Slim and some of their other family members Marlene headed back to the hospital to be with her one and only child who seemed to be so important to her now.

Bogus Azz Hood Chick/ PattiCake Taylor

Marlene sat at the end of Cola's bed and began to talk and apologize for allowing the streets to come between them when she was younger and for allowing Jose to come between them now. "I was pissed and holding on to the fact that you had stayed in the system and not come home after I had gotten myself together but I understand now". Marlene continued to rave on and on about this and that, tears was running down her face. As she turned to say her last goodbye for the night she noticed tears running down Cola's face. Cola had heard everything Marlene was saying and that was God's way of telling Marlene everything was gonna be alright with her child.

The next day Slim had arrived from Atlanta with a few family members from his side of the family. Cola had a sister and brother that she never knew about. Cola barely knew Slim but had heard lots of not so nice things about him from her mother. Slim talked to Cola as she laid there motionless almost. "Cola baby, I need you to make it, I can't bury two of my children, I already buried one".

Bogus Azz Hood Chick/ PattiCake Taylor

"I just layed your brother too rest last week" Slim said through sobs. "He was killed, these muther fuckers shot up your brother and put the gun in his hand trying to make it look like a suicide". "Dumb muther fuckers gonna put the gun in his right hand, when he left handed all day long". "Baby", Slim said, "I know I haven't been a great father but it's never too late to make amends". "Please Cola, pull through for us, your family, we love you and we want to help you get better", Slim stood up and walked out the room.

Three months had past and Cola was starting to look better although she was still in a coma, she had picked up weight from all the vitamins and steroids the nurse had been feeding her through her I.V tube. Marlene started being at the hospital all day every day. She would bathe Cola, comb her long pretty hair as if she was seven years old again. Marlene had dozed off while reading a magazine when she heard a voice in her head. She knew she was dreaming but when she opened her eyes Cola was staring at her saying momma, "momma is that you"?

Bogus Azz Hood Chick/ PattiCake Taylor 191

Marlene jumped up as if she was at a church shouting and screaming "yes baby it's me". "What the hell happened to me"? Cola asked?

"Oh baby" Marlene said, "it's a long story, let me get the nurse baby".

When Marlene returned back to the room with the nurse Marlene started screaming "she was just woke", "oh my god please". "Please God don't take my one and only" Marlene yelled. "Oh God please".

Marlene ran over to Cola saying wake up baby, "please wake up". Cola opened her eyes and said "momma I'm woke", "I'm just having a hard time keeping my eyes open".

Marlene fell to her knee's in prayer.

The nurse informed Marlene that Cola was on heavy medication and that it may take a few days for Cola to be aware. The nurse told Marlene she needed to leave the room so that the doctor could do a examine on Cola.

Two weeks later Cola was released from the hospital and

Bogus Azz Hood Chick/ PattiCake Taylor

Marlene was throwing Cola a welcome home party. Everybody wanted to come because everybody knew Marlene could throw some parties.

When Marlene threw a party you felt like you was still partying a week later. Cola met Malik at her coming home party, he was fine, he dressed nice and smelled very good.

After a couple months of dating Cola finally invited him over. Since Marlene was out of town with her new man. Malik and Cola could be alone. Cola was hot in the ass and she knew Malik was gonna tap her ass real good. Cola went out of her way to make sure everything was on point. She made her bubble bath, had candles, her smell good and just a thong.

Malik arrived and Cola opened the door with a smile. Cola escorted him to kitchen where she had cooked a soul food fest just for him. "Enjoy your meal" she said "and when you're done go to my room and get comfortable I'll be there shortly".

Cola made sure to get all her hot spots three or four times, she wanted to make sure her pussy was on point. Malik was smelling good and it turned Cola on even more. She was ready and willing to do whatever. Cola entered her bedroom after getting out the tub.

Malik had gotten comfortable alright, he just took his shoes off and got in the bed with all his clothes on. They laid up watching television, until they both fell asleep. When they woke up it was a brand new day.

Cola smiled as she cooked breakfast, she complimented Malik on how he was a true gentlemen. Cola invited him over for another night, she knew tonight would be on and popping.

Malik arrived at Cola's crib after work wanting seconds of her home cooked meal. This time Cola made something simple, fried chicken with pasta and a big glass of kool-aid. Cola ran the shower water for Malik and when he was done she headed to the shower. Get as comfortable as you like she yelled to him. When Cola return to her bedroom she had the shit face because Malik had put all his clothes back on after the shower and was in the bed under the cover.

Bogus Azz Hood Chick/ PattiCake Taylor

"Nigga" Cola screamed loud as ever, "you gay or something"? "Get your shit and get your faggot ass out my house".

"How in the hell you gonna lay up with a fine bitch like me two nights in a row with all your damn clothes on after I said get comfortable". "You just got out the shower and you put your nasty ass work clothes back on and got in my clean bed". "Yeah you a faggot, and I thought you were just a gentlemen".

Six months had passed and Cola was looking better than ever. She was twenty one and living the good life with her sugar daddy Arthur Berry. Arthur made sure she didn't want for nothing. He had gotten her a nice two bedroom apartment, bought her a nice truck and kept her with money in her pocket. Cola had her body back it was better then ever because Arthur made sure of that by getting Cola a personal trainer. Cola even upgraded her Walgreens make-up to MAC make up. Cola's face was flawless. That Mac make-up was the shit, you couldn't even tell that Cola had scars in her face. Black people weren't

Bogus Azz Hood Chick/ PattiCake Taylor

hip to Mac but Cola loved it, right down to her lip gloss "Gloss ME Up" by PattiCake Taylor, Cola grabbed lots of samples since it wasn't on the market yet. Arthur and every other nigga loved the way Cola wore her lip gloss.

They really enjoyed the definition of her lips and even more so when they shined like she had been sucking on some greasy chicken.

Cola was happier than ever. She wasn't trying to mess up her good thang but Arthur had an issue with keeping his penis hard and he didn't eat pussy so he wasn't holding it down in the bedroom. That time had come when Cola started craving for some D I C K and it wasn't nothing Arthur could do.

Cola met Yamo while cruising in her truck down the avenue at a stop light.

Later that night Cola met up with Yamo at the Dirty Inn motel hoping he would knock her back out. All she wanted was a fuck, he was fine and he could get it Cola thought as she drove down Independence blvd to the motel.

Bogus Azz Hood Chick/ PattiCake Taylor

Cola and Yamo was getting it, he knocked that fire out her back then made love to her as if she was his one and only. They were all cuddled up when they heard a knock on the motel door.

"OMG", Cola scream when Yamo open the door, it was Arthur standing there with fire in his eyes. Arthur had paid Yamo to trail Cola, get his mack on and try to take her to bed, which was easier then Arthur thought it would be. Arthur thought Cola wouldn't fall for the dick bait over his money but she did.

In a blink of an eye Cola lost all her shit, her crib, her truck and most importantly her self respect. Cola was sick over what had happen, she had did the dummy without thinking but she bounced back quick when she thought of a way to use what she got.

Cola took all the money she had saved up over the course that her and Arthur was together. She knew a rainy day would come and it did. Cola left the Dirty Inn motel after a week and

Bogus Azz Hood Chick/ PattiCake Taylor 197

founded herself a one bedroom apartment. The only furniture she had at the moment was an air mattress that she purchased. Luckily the last tenant left a few things she could use.

Tasteful Entertainment was Cola's new job of the season outbound home private dancing for your pleasure.

Cola made a mental note to herself as ideas came afloat to use white men only because black men were cheap as hell. She learned that the hard way at the Pole in the Wall.

Tasteful Entertainment started off booming for Cola, so booming that she decided to recruit some ladies to help her along the way. Cola called herself (TasteFul) and she added two more ladies to her entertainment. Their names were (Waterfall) and (Mouthlalicious). This trio of ladies were as bad as they come and the white men made it known by their cash flow.

Cola meet Kychelle and Kitanna at the Hilton hotel downtown Chicago. They were hot looking sisters who made their money together and played together if the price was right.

Bogus Azz Hood Chick/ PattiCake Taylor 198

Cola named Kychelle (Waterfall) because she heard she was a squitter during sex and Kitanna (Mouthlalicious) because Cola's very own client told her she was reckless with her blow job. Money was so good that Cola flipped her another truck in no time.

She made sure to get personalized plates so she could rub it in Arthur's face that she was doing good. Cola furnished her one bedroom very well. There was no need for her to move because she was barley home. Cola's little business kept her busy.

Cola headed for the shower, she was treating the ladies to a night out on the town and it was on. The ladies went to one of the hottest night clubs on Michigan ave "Shab's Poppin". They were having a great time, as the DJ pumped the speakers with Luke's doo-doo brown song. Cola snapped out and started screaming that's my muther fucking song. She ran from the back of the club heading to the stage and fell face first to the stage, all eyes were on her and she was embarrassed.

Bogus Azz Hood Chick/ PattiCake Taylor 199

Cola wanted to give them something to talk about other then her falling and busting her shit so she begin to pump the floor. She started doing the cry baby dance, and nigga's begin to get excited when they saw Cola ass pumping the floor. Cola took control of the dance floor and when it was all said and done Cola made five hundred dollars thanks to the trio act she added.

Mouthlalicious ran into a friend while the trio was sipping on their drinks. Beauty was her name but it should've been Beast. she was knocking the door down at three hundred plus pounds, braces, and a two dollar weave. Mouthlalicious began to run her mouth about Cola's business to Beauty and before she knew it she found herself on the floor from a forceful punch by Cola. "Bitch" Cola yelled, "don't be telling my damn business, I don't know this trick she could be the police. Cola was going on and on and in midsentence she thought about Tom and his nasty fantasies and them dollars.

Tom was one of Cola's clients who wanted something

Bogus Azz Hood Chick/ PattiCake Taylor 200

unusual. He paid Cola six hundred dollars just to play with herself and lick her own cum from her orgasm. Cola wasn't tripping, "tasteful is the name and making this money is the game, it's as easy as one, two, three". "Oh Tom, you want me to blow your ass, that's gonna be twenty five hundred dollars go take a shower please" Cola would tell him.

Business was good and booming as usual. Most men would call and request Waterfall, the thing she could do as she squirts from her pussy was a big turn on for the customers. After one of Waterfall's private shows the customer didn't want to pay his extra bill and when Waterfall begin to snap off he busted out with his badge and a gun arrested her after he got his fuck on and busted his nut. Thankfully he was a dumb ass, Waterfall hadn't showered yet so she knew it would be a case won.

After Waterfall was let out of jail free she was all smiles until she was hit with another bad situation at home with her other sister Chyvia.

Chyvia was in a very abusive relationship and it took a

wrong turn when Chyvia killed herself after telling her daughter she was tired of getting beat for breakfast, lunch, and dinner.

Waterfall snapped out, she couldn't deal with the grief and she killed her sister's boyfriend.

Now she was sitting in jail for a murder charge with a sentence of twenty five years to life at twenty one years old, leaving her five children behind for the system to take care of. Her oldest was seven and her youngest baby is only one years old.

A month later Cola ran into an old friend sort of Dimples. Dimples was the light skinned bitch that Cola met at gay pride a couple of years ago. Dimples did a double take as she saw Cola getting out her truck at Ever Black Mall. Dimple walked right up to Cola and slapped the shit out of her without saying a word.

"What the fuck, bitch I know you didn't just slap me" Cola said in a rage. Cola jumped out her stiletto heels and went

Bogus Azz Hood Chick/ PattiCake Taylor 202

ham on Dimples, then out of no where Dimples just bust out crying and when she looked up at Cola she snapped off again. "Bitch why the fuck you got on heels and makeup I thought you were a stud" Dimples said in anger. Cola laughed, "I never said I was a stud, I just had a boyish look going on". "It was my image at that time. "Anyways it was nice of you to slap me and get your ass beat but I must go shopping now", Cola turned around and picked up her heels and walked away.

    Business had been good for Cola but she started losing a lot of clients when word got out that Waterfall was in prison and was no longer working for Tasteful Entertainment. Waterfall was Cola's money maker and Cola was starting to feel the after effect of losing money in her pocket.

    Cola decided to go out for a drink, she was so stressed out. Clients weren't calling like they use to and her money flow was getting lower by the day.

    As Cola drove down Cicero ave to go to Patti's place she saw her mom ex-boyfriend Jose. Cola pulled over to get the attention of two hypes that was on the corner. She walked over to the hypes and before you knew it, Jose was getting his head bashed in with Cola's crow bar. Cola walked back to her truck, look on for a few more minutes and was happy that all she had to do was pay the hypes twenty five dollars apiece to take care of her dirty work.

Patti's Place was a little hole in the wall club. Patti's be on and poppin' though, it was crowded every weekend. Those hole in the wall clubs always be the best. As Cola was walking to Patti's, this fat ass nigga was trying to holla at her.

Cola waved him off at first, until he said "I'm Stuff baby, can I be your teddy bear"?.

Cola laughed at that thought. Stuff was fine to be heavy, Cola smiled and said "Stuff huh that's cute, real cute". "By the way I'm Tasteful", Cola said still smiling, I mean Cola.

Cola and Stuff walked into the club together acting as if they had been a couple for years. Stuff and Cola realized they had a lot in common and Cola was feeling Stuff's persona.

Bogus Azz Hood Chick/ PattiCake Taylor 204

As Stuff and Cola was leaving the club Stuff ran into a few home boys and they decided to head down to the all niter Steak and egg diner on their motorcycles. Stuff asked Cola if she wanted to ride out with him. She said no and told him to holla back later.

Cola was tripping, she couldn't believe she had yet again gave someone her real name.

A week had past and Stuff hadn't called Cola yet, Cola was a little upset about that. "I guess you can't miss what you ain't never had" Cola mumble to herself. "It's all good".

Cola noticed some new tenants moving into the building she stayed in. It turned out to be a mother and her two daughters Silver and Gold was the daughters name and they momma called herself Platinum.

These sisters were beyond ghetto, they were new bitches to the block and that didn't make a difference to the nigga's in the hood that they were ghetto or ghetto looking. Silver and Gold were twins but you couldn't tell, Silver was dark as tar

Bogus Azz Hood Chick/ PattiCake Taylor

with blonde weave in her hair, black liner on her lips with red lipstick and Gold was lighter than a light bulb, with fire red hair weave in her head, black liner on her lip and pink lipstick, what a bad combination. These bitches had body on top of body though and Cola wanted them on the Tasteful Entertainment… team.

Cola was broke as hell and she needed to find a way to make some easy fast quick money and she knew Gold would be her money maker. Cola decided she would still do the private dancing but all that other shit for her would be dead because she refuse to go to jail. She would just make the other girls do strange thangs for that change.

Al B, is what the chicken heads on the block called him, he thought he could sing but he really sounded like a chipmunk, he was fine as hell though. Al B tried to holla at Cola but she blew him off, "nigga you never tried to holla at me when I was fat, now a bitch lost weight and looking good you want to try and holla". "I remember you nigga, you from off Homan and

Bogus Azz Hood Chick/ PattiCake Taylor 206

Walnut, no thank you partner" Cola said.

Al B laughed a little and turned his attention to Gold and Gold was all smiles. "Gat damn it" Cola said out loud, "These niggas know they know how to get on a bitch bad side with these light skinned bitches".

"But hell I knew it" Cola said, "I knew these nigga's was gonna be all in Gold's face, that's cool though". "I'll just be friends with Silver" Cola mumble.

A month had past, Cola and Silver were best of friends. They was kicking it every day after they got off work. Silver had hooked Cola up with a job at Chi-Town City Suites as a front desk agent right off the magnificent mile. Cola was loving it, even more so when she came up with an idea to have the men come to the job. Cola had to find a way to tell Silver so they could work hand in hand together.

Cola enjoyed her front desk agent job for the most part but she couldn't stand the new human resources manger. The bitch was white but thought she was black, she was dating black men and thought she had a black woman's booty but really she was wearing a booty pad.

Cola couldn't take Amy white ass nagging no more. So she paid this homeless man to rob Amy after work and to knock her front teeth out.

Cola laughed at that thought, "I bet that white bitch won't be smiling at no more black men".

It was payday and Cola was feeling good, Amy had gotten robbed and rushed to the hospital.

It was lunch time, Cola decided to take Silver out since it was her that got her the job. Cola had to find a way to tell Silver about Tasteful Entertainment. After seeing that her check was only six hundred and forty dollars after taxes, she knew something was gonna have to give. Cola told Silver about a made up friend and the Tasteful Entertainment business. Cola was shocked at Silver's response and that she would be down. Cola finally revealed that the friend was her. Silver laughed at that thought and told Cola she could have just kept it real.

Bogus Azz Hood Chick/ PattiCake Taylor 208

After lunch they headed back to work, so they could punch out for the day. They then headed back to Cola's crib so they could form a plan on how to get their hustle on. Cola had to get her a pre-paid cell phone. She couldn't allow these men to call her work number for the business she was doing.

It was funny how Cola had forgotten about her old crew until she got a call from beast, that's what Cola called Beauty behind her back. Cola had put Beauty on a few dates when the client asked for a plus sized woman. Beauty was crying and screaming like a mad woman in the phone. Cola tried to calm her down, "what's going on" Cola asked? "I would rather come over" Beauty said.

Beauty arrived within fifteen minutes still crying and giving Cola a letter she was clueless about. "What the fuck is this" Cola asked "and can you shut the fuck up, I can't understand nothing you saying or crying about". Beauty gave Cola this ugly look and then she began remember....

"Remember a few months ago when you sent me on that call

to the Under Ground motel". "Yeah" Cola said, "that client I told you that was super, super fine and gave Mothlalicious a thousand dollars to suck him off and fuck her in the ass". "Yes that's him" Beauty cried, "well read this letter I got" Beauty cried more. Cola snatched the letter open.

"Hey baby girl, glad you were able to come to the motel today, this is Montay". "I had a wonderful time when I was in Chicago with you". "Do you remember the fun we had"? "OKAY" Cola said "what's wrong with this letter, it sounds good so far".

Beauty snatched the letter back from Cola and she continued to read. "Remember how you sucked me so good and you allowed me to fuck you in every hole, Mmmmm, how your pussy went deep like an ocean". "Well baby girl with that in mind, I decided to send you a gift, turn this letter over and read with a smile"!

As Beauty turned the letter over, she began to cry again. She was getting on Cola's last nerve.

Bogus Azz Hood Chick/ PattiCake Taylor 210

Cola took the letter and began to read some more. Cola started yelling, "oh my god", "what in the hell", she grabbed Beauty. "I'm so, so sorry, I know this got to be a joke". Cola reread the letter again out loud, "tell Tasteful thank you for sending you and in return my gift to you baby girl is years of sickness, welcome to the wonderful world of AIDS".

Cola cried out with Beauty. Cola was crying but secretly she was happy that she sent Mouthlalicious for that thousand dollars and got half the money instead of going herself. Through her tears, Cola said, "I guess I better call Mouthlalicious so you both can go to the clinic".

Over the next few weeks, things was going great for Cola. She was still working at the hotel and she was still dancing on the side, that's it, that's all. Cola vowed not to sleep with none of the client's no matter how much more money they offer her. Things started to boil for the twins Silver and Gold. Gold was upset that Silver was spending more time with Cola than her.

Bogus Azz Hood Chick/ PattiCake Taylor 211

Gold was so mad that she started a rumor in the building that Cola was a dyke and was trying to dyke on her sista, hoping Silver would dislike Cola and not be her friend anymore. It made Gold even madder when Cola heard the rumor and didn't get mad but got checked by Cola instead.

"Bitch" Cola caught Gold coming in the building, "you think you did something by calling me a dyke"? "I done been with plenty of bitches and I guarantee I'm gonna be with Silver too". "I'm gonna show you a dyke, you high yellow looking like a raccoon around the eye bitch" said Cola as she walked off laughing. "I will get the last laugh bitch kno dat" said Cola.

Gold had the shit face when she founded out Cola and Silver had starting such a nasty rumor about her. They told everybody that she had crabs and she gave it to Al B.

Business started to slow down at the hotel and since Cola was the last to get hired she suffer from hour cuts. She went from full time five days a week to two days a week. Cola wondered what she was gonna do. Her idea for the clients

Bogus Azz Hood Chick/ PattiCake Taylor 212

to come to the hotel didn't work out either. Cola had quit her job. Sixteen hours a week wasn't worth coming to work in her opinion. She needed to find a way to get her cash flow back up and quick. Cola was sitting in her truck in a day dream, when she heard a voice, say "what up ma"?

Cola's neck whipped hard as hell, when she thought it was Daddy B's voice she heard. She looked and did a double take. "Daddy B, I thought you was dead". "Excuse me Ma, my name not Daddy B, I'm Shaleek".

"I love me some chocolate dark skinned woman, what's your name"? "I'm Tomica", Cola said to him, "and right now I don't have time for your bullshit".

Cola started her truck and headed home.

As Cola entered her key she heard her house phone ringing. She broke her neck to answer it. "Hello", she said! "Hey baby" the caller said in his deep voice. "Who the fuck is this"? Cola spat! "Calm down baby, it's your teddy bear Stuff". "Stuff who"? Cola spat into the phone. "Oh now you don't remember me huh"? Stuff asked "hell nawl", "I give you my number how long ago and you just now calling me, boy fly with that shit" Cola said.

"Let me explain" Stuff said, "I was on lockdown for a minute".

"Yeah with a bitch" Cola yelled. "Nawl baby I was in jail" Stuff said.

"Whatever" Cola said.

"I will call you back I just got into the crib and I need to shower". "Aiight" Stuff said and Cola hung up.

Cola showered, made her a t.v dinner and flopped down on the couch, trying to figure out a way to pay her bills, and using her body wasn't an option. Cola wasn't trying to go to jail for bullshit.

Cola called Stuff back just to see what he was on. Cola wasn't paying much attention to his conversation until she heard five thousand dollars. She choked on her kool-aid as she screamed "five thousand dollars for what"?

Bogus Azz Hood Chick/ PattiCake Taylor 214

"All you gotta do Stuff said, is take some work up to one of my homeboys in Taylorland correctional center for one month and then the money is yours".

"Oh hell nawl nigga", Cola replied "you gonna have to pay me first before I do some shit like that". "What the fuck I look like risking my life for some maybes, nigga I was born at night, not last night, do I look like boo, boo the fool or a fool". "You crazy then a muther fucker if you think I'm just gonna go off your word that you gonna pay me nigga please".

"ha-ha" Stuff laughed.

"Ha-ha my damn ass" then Cola hung up. Cola stepped outside to get some air. Something that she hadn't done in a long time. Cola had so much going on that she decided to go for a ride, when she noticed her truck was gone. "Gat damn it" Cola screamed out loud, "these muther fuckers done repo my shit". Cola ran into the house and called her finance company going off about her truck and why they repo her shit.

Ms. Johnson the rep replied, "you are four months behind,

that's why we repossessed your truck and unless you have eighteen hundred dollars there's nothing I can do to help you".

"Thank you" Cola said with an attitude, mad she hadn't paid her truck note in a few months because her funds were low as hell. All Cola could think of at that moment was Stuff and that five thousand dollars.

"Who the fuck is it"?

Cola yelled as the knock at the door scared the shit out of her.

"It's Silver girl open the damn door"! Cola opened the door, "what's going on girl" Cola said to Silver. "Oh girl," Silver was laughing" I met this nigga name Heno, he fine as hell and his homie Keno, wanted me to hook him up with someone as fine as me".

Cola busted out laughing to the point she started crying. "What the hell is that funny"? Silver asked with this evil glare in her eyes. "Oh nothing" Cola said as she continue to laugh, "I just thought of something that was funny but it's nothing major so calm your ass down Silver". Cola laughed some more to herself as she thought Silver wasn't no where near fine. She wasn't even cute and that blonde ass weave didn't do her no justice.

Silver and Cola headed downstairs to meet the guys once Cola got dolled up, it was no way Cola was gonna go meet a man looking a hot mess.

"Oh yeah" Cola whispered to Silver "Keno is fine". "DAMN" "He so chocolate and from what I can see he may be sexy, he need to get his ass out the car though".

"Hey guys", Cola and Silver said at the same time. "Heno this my fine as me friend Cola" Silver said. Heno's smile got wide as he kissed Cola on her hand. Cola blushed, "hey Heno" said Cola.

Silver looked with a what the fuck is you doing look at Heno. "Excuse me" Silver said "Keno this is my fine as me friend Cola". "Hey baby girl" Keno said. Cola just looked at him, "you not gonna get out the car, I'm not impress how fly your ride is, I would have been more impress if you would have got out and greeted me as Heno did". "No problem ma, I'll get out" Keno said.

Keno pop his trunk and Heno pulled out a wheel chair. Keno open the driver door and transfer himself to the wheel chair. Cola looked, Silver looked. "Oh hell nawl I'm good" Cola said. Cola turned around and walked back towards the building. Cola entered her crib pissed, "what the fuck was Silver thinking she a stupid bitch".

There was a knock at Cola's door as she was in mid thought. Cola acted as if she didn't hear the door, and turned on her music and laid down.

"What's up Cola", Silver said to her as Cola put her clothes in the washer in the laundry room. Cola ignored her still salty at what happen last week with Keno.

"Bitch I know you hear me"! Silver screamed. Cola turned around fast ass hell, "Bitch" "who the hell you calling a bitch, ugly hoe". Silver looked sideways, "damn Cola" Silver said,

Bogus Azz Hood Chick/ PattiCake Taylor 218

"I meant the friendly bitch and you fucking tripping and I ain't ugly". "Well I'm not your bitch" Cola said, "and yeah your ass ugly and don't you ever call me a bitch again, now get the fuck out my face".

"But Cola" Silver tried to say, "but Cola my whole entire ass now go bitch".

Silver left the laundry room.

"Damn" some girl said as she laughed from the other side of the laundry room, "you just snapped the fuck out and it wasn't even that serious".

"Shut the fuck up talking to me" Cola snapped.

"Hold up with that"! "There's no need to be upset with me, I ain't the one that made you mad so chill". "Now, how you doing"? "I'm Devotion, I just move in the building I'm from Pine Bluff, I'm new to Chicago and I don't know anybody here, and I'm trying to meet some new people".

"Oh" Cola said, "hi and I'm not looking for no new friends, bitches get on my nerves and I can't stand phony jealous ass

Bogus Azz Hood Chick/ PattiCake Taylor

hoes"." I hear ya girl, I'm none of the above you mention, so if you ever want to kick it, I'm in unit 508" Devotion said. Cola said "ok" "ummm, do you got a car"? "Yeah" Devotion said with a smile. "Well alrighty maybe we will go to the club or something". Devotion starting laughing, "giiiiiiirl, I'm only nineteen"! "Stop lying" Cola said you look ever bit of twenty five with all those titties. Devotion was alright looking, brown skinned, big hazel eyes, long hair, big titties and no ass.

As Devotion laughed she told Cola to holla back, she had to get to her KFC job. "Aiiiight girl" Cola said, "make that money, and if it's not enough steal it". "Just joking" Cola laughed, and they went their separate ways.

Cola decided to give Stuff a call, she needed money and needed it fast because she wanted her truck back and needed to catch up on some past due bills.

Stuff returned Cola's call two hours later, as they came up with an agreement that he would pay her half of the five thousand when she pick up the package and she would get the

Bogus Azz Hood Chick/ PattiCake Taylor 220

other half, after she drop off the package. Stuff told Cola they would meet up in a couple of days and be prepared to stuff her pussy with balloons full of drugs.

"Boy fly" Cola told Stuff, "I'm gonna put that shit in my panties".

Saturday came and Cola took the three hours bus ride to Joliet IL, to go to Taylorland Correctional Center.

Cola stomach turned knots as the bus pulled up to the prison.

Cola walked in took a number and waited.

"Number seven" the correctional officer called.

Cola got up and went to the front desk handed the C-O her information and ask for the inmate. Cola started to cry, the C-O asked what was wrong. Cola said nothing and cry a little harder, through her fake tears she asked for inmate Tyris Gant K-12121.

"I'm sorry Ms. Johnson but your name not on the visitor list so you can't visit him today" the C-O said. "what" Cola yelled "that's impossible, his ass knew I was coming".

Bogus Azz Hood Chick/ PattiCake Taylor

Cola flew through her door, slammed it as if someone was there to feel her pain, she broke her neck to call Stuff, pissed she had to wait an hour for another pace bus, then take another three hours to get home.

"Hello" Cola said angrily in the phone.

Stuff must have been waiting for Cola's call because his first words were I had to test you first. "I had to be sure I could trust you and you wouldn't go to the police on me" he said.

"What the fuck Stuff why would you put my muther fucking life at risk like that for some bull shit". "Oh well nigga, I got your shit, and if you don't give me the other half of my money I will go to the police" Cola spat.

"Stupid bitch, do what you gotta do" Stuff laughed into the phone, "it's dumb bitches like you that will do anything for money".

"You can have that little chump change I gave you, I bet my boy ten thousand you would fall for the bait, so twenty five hundred ain't shit I triple that shit and as far as the drugs goes

Bogus Azz Hood Chick/ PattiCake Taylor

what drugs hoe, I gave you twenty balloons full of baking soda". "click" and Stuff hung up in Cola's face.

Cola sat there on the couch looking dumb founded, she couldn't believe her ears and she was pissed. Cola was heated, as she kept redialing Stuff number all she kept getting was his voicemail.

After three days of Cola calling Stuff he changed his phone number he was tired of Cola and her bogus azz hood chick voicemails.

Cola decided she would write an anonymous letter to Tyris Gant warden "if that fat ass nigga tried to get me to take drugs, I'm fucking sure he's gonna get somebody else" Cola said to herself as she continue to write, "I'll fix that nigga, Ha"!! Cola said with a giggled. She finished her letter then laid down to take a nap.

Cola had to be tired, she didn't wake up until she heard a knock at the door when she looked at the clock it was noon the next day.

Bogus Azz Hood Chick/ PattiCake Taylor 223

Cola looked through her peep hole to see Silver standing there, Cola opened the door and asked "what's up" as she walked away from the door. Silver stood at the door crying and looking crazy. Cola asked "what's up" again with a little attitude in her voice.

"Oh nothing major" Silver said, it's just Gold and I got into it over my mother. "Oh" Cola said back as sweet as she could "can you come back later, I'm trying to sleep and I really don't feel good" Cola said.

Silver just stood there dumb founded for a second and then out of know where she asked "what would you do if someone was doing something to you all your life and you was just tired of it". Cola gave Silver a blank stared, "I'm lost what do you mean" Cola asked? "Please promise me you want say nothing Cola".

"I promise Silver, now what is it".

"My mother has been molesting me as far as I can remember I was at least four when she started". "I didn't understand what she was doing then, but as I got older I understood what she was doing was wrong".

"WHAT" Cola yelled, "I'm about to go kill that bitch". "No!! please don't Cola" "I need a favor from you though" Silver said. "Can I please stay with you for a little while"? "I will help you with your bills".

That's all Cola needed to hear as she said yes and hugged Silver to comfort her. Silver hugged Cola tight a little too tight Cola thought to herself.

Over the next few months things were going great with Cola and Silver they had their late nights when they would stay up and talk, eat popcorn and watch movies. Things were going better than Cola thought they would go. Things were going so good Silver started paying all the bills.

As Cola laughed to herself in thought, how she had Silver nose wide open "I guess she never had a good tongue bath by a nigga before". "I be showering that bitch with my tongue". "I often heard ugly bitches had the best pussy though". "Hell that shit can't be true, I know I ain't ugly and I got some fye pussy" Cola mumbled to herself. "Cola"!!, Silver knocked Cola out of her thought. "Yeah" Cola said, "I'm headed to the store I'll be back" Silver said loudly.

Cola couldn't get over the fact, how she love women. Cola and Silver had become a couple after one night when Cola had to pee and entered the bathroom to see Silver naked and her banging body. Silver may have been ugly, but she was thick her body was on fire and she had that stuck pussy.

Every time you stick your tongue in Silver pussy it would catch like a ziplock. Nigga's and bitches love some stuck pussy. Cola made sure she had that on double lock, she refused to let her good money thang get away. Cola was gonna go all out to do what was needed to keep a bitch like Silver happy.

Cola headed to the treasure play house sex store, she wanted to spice the bedroom up for Silver. Cola had been thinking about getting one of those things Smoove had pull out for her to suck.

Bogus Azz Hood Chick/ PattiCake Taylor 226

Cola stopped to pick up a few groceries on her way home. She wanted to cook Silver her favorite cat fish and lasagna. Cola entered her crib, running straight to the kitchen because her bags were heavy. As soon as Cola entered the kitchen she dropped all the food on the floor.

"What the fuck" Cola yelled!!

"What the fuck this bitch doing in my muther fucking house Silver". "Get this bitch out my shit Silver and I mean now" Cola was yelling at the top of her lungs.

The house guest began yelling at Silver too. "Get your shit Silver and let's go and let's go right now this crazy bitch killed my friend Gia".

"Wait hold up both of you and shut the fuck up please" Silver was now yelling.

"Baby" Silver said to Cola, "do you know my cousin Starr"?

"Yeah" Cola said "and this bitch gotta go and for the record I didn't killed nobody, fuck I look like goofy". "Now get the fuck out my crib, and Silver you can ride along too if it's a problem" Cola spat.

"I'm fucking confused cousin what the hell going on" Silver ask? "I'll tell you" Starr began, "your bitch was salty that she was fucking me and this girl she killed name Gia, she saw us together at pride and found out Gia and I was fucking too". "Cola and I was fucking and Cola snapped the fuck out". "So you can either ride out with me or stay, either way I'm heading to the police department to report this bitch" Starr said. Cola grabbed Starr by the throat "bitch I told you I didn't killed anybody"

"I told your dumb ass that, if the police come looking for me I will kill you mark my words" Cola spat. Starr was scared to death as she ran out Cola's crib.

Silver ran behind Starr confused and trying to put together this puzzle Starr was talking about. Silver shook Starr and asked what the hell was going on? Starr was talking in a panic.

"Look Silver" Starr said, "that bitch in there Cola or whatever you called her is crazy and she killed my friend".

Bogus Azz Hood Chick/ PattiCake Taylor

"She crazy as fuck" Starr said "and if you want to live you will move out that bitch psycho"!!

Silver just started laughing as she told Starr she was crazy, "remember cousin you get a check on the first" Silver continue to laughed.

"Cola ain't killed nobody and how you so sure it was her anyways"? Silver asked. "Don't believe me Silver, I don't give two fucks, but I swear if anything happens to you I will go to the police" Starr said "know that I love you Silver we blood but unless you stop being friends with that Cola girl, if that's her real name you won't see me around her no more". Starr got on the elevator and was out.

Meanwhile back at the crib Cola had went hay wire, fucking up all her all shit. When Silver entered the apartment she couldn't believe her eyes as she tried to talk to Cola. Things just got worst Cola cussed and fussed "for Chicago to be such a big city it is a small fucking ass world" Cola mumble to herself.

"Come here baby" Silver said sweetly. "Get the fuck out my

crib" Cola yelled back. Silver looked at Cola as if she was crazy and wondered if her cousin Starr was right about Cola being psycho. Silver picked up her purse and headed for the door.

"What the fuck" Cola scream to herself "this dumb bitch then let this bitch into my crib". "Starr dumb ass know where I stay now". "What the fuck I'm I going to do"? "Calm down Cola" Cola continue to talked to herself, "think girl shit". Cola kept going in circle's, "I need a fucking getaway" Cola mumbled.

"No hell nawl I didn't kill nobody this bitch ain't go run me out my crib". "I'll kill her if that bitch ass dyke goes to the cops". "Bitch I hate you" Cola screamed aloud.

Cola sat there for an hour or so talking to herself before going to sleep. She was awaken when she heard a knock at the door. Cola went to look out the peep hole and gasp for air when she seen the po-po at her door. Cola began to panic, she pissed on herself as she sweated bullets, she heard the knock again and then an officer said "shit we at the wrong door".

Cola was feeling like she was losing her mind she headed for the shower as she thought maybe she would move to Atlanta where all the black people go once they leave Chicago.

After Cola showered she decided she needed a much needed walk before she lost her mind. She threw on an oversize sweat shirt, jogging pants, her shades, gloves and a baseball cap and was on her way.

Cola pushed for the elevator and got on when it arrived Cola was still in raged and heated she was talking to herself she hadn't even realize the elevator had stop on the next floor and pick someone up. When Cola looked up she realized Starr was on the elevator with her.

Cola just lost it. Cola started choking Starr, as Starr begged for her life through her chokes. The elevator reached the first floor Cola hurried and pushed the tenth floor when the elevator stopped on the first floor.

Bogus Azz Hood Chick/ PattiCake Taylor 231

Cola dragged Starr off the elevator toward the fire escape. Starr tried her best to fight Cola off, but Cola had gotten the best of her.

"I hope they ain't fix this alarm yet" Cola mumble. "Yes this alarm light still out". Cola open the fire escape door with the force of Starr body. Cola knocked Starr over the fire escape banister to her death. Cola ran as fast as she could up the stairs to the thirteen floor she showered again, dried her body with her blow dryer threw on her pj's as if she never had left her apartment. "Bitch" Cola mumbled, "I bet you wish you didn't stop at your auntie house now". BAM!

"Thank God I grabbed my gloves even though they were Stuff glove's". "I stole them out his car the last time we seen each other hell they were name brand and I wanted them" Cola laughed to herself. Cola laid back down in relief she didn't have to move for the time being.

Later that night Silver came back to the crib to check on Cola being that she was a little scared she asked her sister Gold to go upstairs with her. Silver knocked on the door instead she was scared to used her keys.

Cola opened the door she couldn't do nothing but laugh Gold had dye her hair blonde and her damn eyebrows blonde too. "What the hell" Cola laughed some more "you must trying to be a wigger or something". "What the hell is a wigger Gold asked"? "A black person trying to be white stupid" Cola replied, "anyway what the fuck y'all want"?

"I just came to check on you baby" Silver said so sweet. "What the fuck for"? Cola yelled at Silver.

"Excuse me Gold added her two cents in". "Why in the hell you calling Cola baby" Silver?

"Oh didn't your little sister tell you we fucking now" Cola grin, "I guess not huh". "Well I'm trying 2 relax a bitch got cramps so get the fuck out" said Cola!

Silver and Gold got up and left out not wanting to argue with Cola. As they stood and waited for the elevator, Gold asked a billion question trying to figured what the hell Cola was talking about her sister and her was fucking.

The elevator open "what's up Twins". "I think your cousin well she look like y'all cousin that girl I seen you with earlier today something happen, they got police and everything in the alley they been out there an hour now trying to get clues on what happen".

"An hour Silver screamed. "Yeah an hour" he said. "They trying to figured out who they got in that body bag".

Silver flew down those thirteen flights of stairs with Gold on her heels. The police wouldn't let anyone close to the body.

Silver screamed "I heard that might be my cousin let me muther fucking see".

The police ignored Silver and continued his task. Silver and Gold was talking wondering who was dude and how he knew that might be their cousin in that body bag. "I ain't never seen him before said Gold.

"I don't know him either" Silver said with a slight attitude, but I'm going to find out if that's my muther fucking cousin

Bogus Azz Hood Chick/ PattiCake Taylor 234

Starr or not.

Three days later, The twins and the rest of the family founded out that it was indeed Starr that was in the alley dead in the body bag. Silver wreck her brain trying to find out what happened and who was that dude that mention it could have been her cousin Starr. Silver wondered if Cola really had something to do with the death of Starr.

As the family made funeral arrangements Silver went into shocked when she overheard Starr mom Pasha say the police said that Starr had to be attacked by a woman although the attacker had on gloves the circle prints around her neck was small. Silver jumped up screaming "noooooooo". "Oh my god no I need some damn air". Gold jumped up behind Silver asking if she wanted her to go with her, Silver said no and left out the door.

Silver climbed six flights of stairs before reaching Cola door. Silver banged on the door with force. When Cola open the door Silver push her way in telling Cola they needed to talk.

Bogus Azz Hood Chick/ PattiCake Taylor 235

"So what's up" Cola said, "make it quick because I'm in a hurry I got shit to do and I don't got time to be wasting it on bullshit".

Silver just stood there staring at Cola then out of no where Silver slapped the shit out of her.

Cola was at dismiss for a hot second asking Silver what fuck was her problem while she returned the favored to a slap to the face. Now crying Silver yelled "you killed my muther fucking cousin that's the fucking problem". Cola looked so dumb founded "what the fuck you talking about Silver" Cola spat?

The police told my auntie Pasha "it had to be a woman who killed her daughter because of the hand print through the gloves and my cousin also told me you was psycho and you killed before". "So tell me did you fucking kill my cousin" Silver yelled at the top of her lungs.

Silver was all in Cola face asking her did she kill her cousin Starr. Cola was getting fed up, she asked Silver to leave nicely.

Bogus Azz Hood Chick/ PattiCake Taylor 236

Silver founded some courage she thought Cola was backing down. "Bitch, I ain't going no were until you tell me what the fuck I want to know".

Cola growing angry of this notion told Silver to leave or else. "Or else what bitch" said Silver. Silver had her hands all up in Cola face "what you gonna do Cola kill me like you did my cousin you dyke bitch" Silver screamed. "Yep" Cola screamed back. Silver eyes got big she started to panic she ran to Cola door trying to exit but it was too late. Cola had Silver around the neck chocking her with a belt.

Cola kept choking Silver until she no longer fought no more. When Cola was done she dragged Silver into her bathroom and waited until the wee hours of the morning taking Silver arms legs and the rest of her body parts to the garage shoot a bag at a time. Cola ran back into the crib making sure she didn't leave no evidence that Silver had been there last night.

A few days later the building janitor found parts of Silver body as he cleaned the garbage shoot out out and saw a blood trail when he opened one of the bags with a bad smell he founded Silver head inside chainsaw off.

Later on that evening police were going door to door asking everyone in sight if they had any information. The only lead the police had at the time was what Gold had told them about the mystery guy who said that maybe there cousin in the alley.

When Cola heard that bit on news she was happy because no one expected her of either crime.

A couple weeks later.. everything had died down and Cola went back to the drawing board. "Where in the hell I'm I gonna get some money to pay my bills" Cola fussed at herself. Cola ran through the few dollars she had gotten from Stuff and Albert.

Two Years Later….

Cola had been working at a work release center that held over three hundred inmates that were on their way home. The inmates had spent some years in prison for varies crimes.

Bogus Azz Hood Chick/ PattiCake Taylor 238

Cola and Oceana one of the female officers had become real cool. They had started messing around with some inmates. The inmates loved Oceana word traveled fast that her booty was super loose and the nigga's was loving how she deep throat. Cola had become involved with a couple of inmates herself Noon was one of them.

Noon was hella fine sexy chocolate. Cola was loving her some Noon she was like his puppet. One evening Cola and Noon got busted having sex in the men restroom in the visitor room after Noon had his sister to come see him as a cover up.

Cola lost her job at the work release center. They shipped Kwame Woods known as Noon back to Taylorland correctional center.

It didn't stop the love birds. Cola was still down for her man and she did all she could to show him she was his hood chick.

Cola had gotten her a little trap of a car with her bogus income tax money so she could drive and see Noon every weekend.

Bogus Azz Hood Chick/ PattiCake Taylor 239

After a few months Noon noticed that Cola would do anything for him. He began to tell Cola he loved her and needed her when he saw Cola eyes lighten up he pop the big question. "Baby" Noon said, "I need you to bring drugs up her to Taylorland so I can take of you while I'm in here". Cola replied "I'm your hood chick daddee I'll do anything for you". He told her to make sure they were bag real good shallow them the night before and take some exlax a few hours later and by the time she come to the prison she should have to shit. Noon told her to go through her own shit to find the drugs and then clean all the plastic bags with soap so he could swallow them before the visit was over.

"Damn it's Saturday again" Cola said with a slight attitude "I love this nigga but I'm tired already going up to this prison".

Noon was a really good guy. He came from a long line of drug dealers he was a hustler and the streets was all he knew. He refused to get a nine to five because street hustle money was the easiest but he understood it came with a price and he didn't give two shit's.

Noon was given Cola some powerful dick before they got busted he had her head, and he knew it. Cola was really feeling Noon and she hoped Noon was feeling her just as much.

After a few more visits Noon started asking Cola to wear a dress. It didn't take long for Noon to learn the ropes of the prison. He wanted to keep Cola nose open.

Noon told Cola they were gonna get their freak on "I love that tight pussy" he would tell her and I don't want no other nigga fucking you.

It had been six months since Noon had gotten sent back to prison.

"Gat damn it" Cola said as she wrote in her journal "I'm tired of playing with my own pussy".

"I guess Noon wanna finger fuck me since he talking about wear a dress on the next visit". "I need some dick shit" Cola closed her journal and went to shower.

Noon had figured out how many times the correctional

officers would check the visitor's room per shift. Noon and one of his homeboys had come up with a fucking plan system they would get fifteen minutes each to fuck they woman.

It was just enough room in between the vending machine for two people to squeeze and get a quick fuck.

You've had to have someone stand in front of the gap of the vending machine for two reasons, one: to protect you from the other visitors and inmates and the other reason so you could sneak out if an correctional officer was coming. No one wanted to get ninety days in the hole if busted. Cola was scared as hell on visiting day.

Noon told Cola about the idea, Cola thoughts went back to the work released when they got busted. Cola was bend over with her ass in the air, her hands on the floor with a slight bent getting it in.

Cola didn't want to get band from the prison and she didn't want Noon to get more prison time. She wanted some dick badly so she put those thoughts behind her and figured they had to do what they had to do.

Watching the first couple had Cola pussy hotter than ever knowing her and her man Noon would be next and she was gonna get that back blown out for at least five minutes.

Noon had some good dick Cola thought but he came way too quick for her.

Fadell was Noon homie name and his girl Shavanika they couldn't wait to get in between them vending machines. Shavanika didn't play she pulled out Fadell dick like it was a lollipop and after ten minutes he busted in her mouth. Fadell was still hard and it was turning Cola the fuck on.

Fadell snatched Shavanika thong to the side and began to bang her like she was his last supper. Cola tried not stare but she couldn't help it. They were turning her on and she couldn't wait for her turn. Noon turned around and seen slob hanging from Cola mouth.

"Bitch" Noon said save that slob for this dick. Cola frowned at that thought she never really was big on sucking dick but she

Bogus Azz Hood Chick/ PattiCake Taylor

loved to eat some pussy.

"Hell yeah that's my nigga" Noon said "making up from last week huh". Fadell couldn't get none because he had a write up.

"How the hell" Cola whisper to Noon "how the hell Shavanika wrap her legs around Fadell waist like that as he hit it from the back". Noon and Cola both had an instant turned on and Noon was looking at Shavanika like he wanted to bang her brains out.

Cola was so turned on that she began to give Noon a hand job. Noon moaned so softly as Shavanika rubbed her titties. Shavanika had Noon dick on ten.

Cola got excited and gave Noon dick a couple of wet mouth slurps since she thought he was so turned on by her hand job.

Fadell and Shavanika had finished and as soon as they step from the vending machine area an correctional officer came to do head count and informed all the visitor's they head to leave due to an emergency lock down.

Cola was pissed off that she had to wait to next visit to get

Bogus Azz Hood Chick/ PattiCake Taylor

some dick. Cola went home horny as a pussy cat in heat. She had to get some dick "hell" she thought "it been fucking six months since I had some dick, that nigga wouldn't know something been up in me". "Mmmmm"... Cola screamed out "I'm cuming, yes I'm cuming, fuck me harder I need this nut bad".

Cola finished getting her nut off she throw her dildo against the wall. "Shit" Cola fussed at herself "I need some real dick". Cola turned over and went to sleep.

Cola had been meeting niggas after niggas but she was feeling Noon so hard she didn't have eyes for no one but him.

Cola waited on the next visitor's day to get some dick. As soon as Cola walked into the visitor's room she told Noon they needed to go first because her pussy was on fire and she couldn't wait another day.

Noon told Fadell to post up. As soon as Fadell did Noon and Cola wasted no time getting in between those vending machines.

Bogus Azz Hood Chick/ PattiCake Taylor 245

Cola pulled out Noon semi hard dick and began to lick on it before she suck the meat off it. Noon wasn't as hard as normal but he made the best of it.

As Noon began to looked at Shavanika play with her pussy under the table Noon got harder then a hammer. Noon took Cola head and started banging it like he was fucking her pussy. he went harder and harder and Cola began to choke but Noon wouldn't stop.

A visitor saw what was going on and went to get the officer that was at the other end of the visitor room. When the officer came Cola was vomiting every where.

The officers noticed ten little blue bags mix in her vomit the Correctional Officer called for backup they snatched Cola off the floor hand cuffed her. Lights out was the last word she heard.

It was six in the morning Cola heard someone screaming "wake up gat damn it, It's the PattiCake Pa Pow Boom Kack Kack Dot Bam morning show where we keep it real all day every day BAM".

Cola jumped up looking crazy she noticed her journal on the floor she picked it up and began to read what she had written and at that moment she knew she had a bad ass dream.

"It's Saturday and sorry Noon" Cola laughed to herself "you want be seeing me today I know that dream gotta be a sign not to come and visit".

Cola sat at her kitchen table eating her eggs and bacon with a muffin. As she wrote in her journal something she started to do when ever she was in deep thought about something. "I know that nigga don't love me" Cola press hard against her paper. "If he did he would've never asked me to bring drugs to him".

"My granny always told me pay attention to your dreams and I am (The End)" Cola closed her journal.

It was about 5:30pm when Cola phone began to ring off the hook. Cola knew it was Noon because the caller I.D said Illinois Correctional.

Noon was hotter than boiling hot water at Cola because she

Bogus Azz Hood Chick/ PattiCake Taylor

was a no show and he already had taken his customers money and spent it on some fresh Nike's and now he had no product to deliver.

After calling for the tenth time and Cola didn't answered Noon hang up and call his other girl after fifteen minutes of talking to her he asked her to call his homeboy crib and block her number because his homeboy girl be tripping.

Cola was in a day dream about what she was gonna tell Noon for her not coming when her phone rang. Cola looked at the phone "who the hell calling me private". Cola snatch the phone up "who the fuck is this calling my phone private" Cola yelled into the phone.

"Yeah bitch" Noon spat back "you fucking with my bread bitch, you dead". "Shavanika baby hang the phone up" said Noon.

Cola went in a rage "I know this nigga didn't just threaten me and had the nerve to have Shavanika call me and call that bitch baby". "She stupid she must forgetten she gave me her

Bogus Azz Hood Chick/ PattiCake Taylor

number on the last visit to Taylorland". "Oh bitch" Cola screamed "you gonna get yours".

Cola paced her floor thinking of a master plan when something great popped in her head Cola laughed so hard "aiiiiight nigga I got something for that ass".

The next day Cola got up and went on Madison and Pulaski to get her a phony I.D. Cola was gonna teach Noon a lesson. "Yep" said Cola as if she was talking to someone "I'm gonna used what I got to get what I want".

One of the correctional officers tried to holla at Cola. Vermaine the Correctional Officer had already given Cola his number months ago.

Vermaine was always in Cola's face when she came to see Noon at the prison. Cola thought this would be the perfect opportunity to call Vermaine and talk to him every day until Friday. She needed his nose open so he wouldn't stared at her I.D too hard. Cola wanted to get through the prison without anyone knowing that she was there.

Bogus Azz Hood Chick/ PattiCake Taylor

The week had flew by it was Friday night and this would be the night Cola would lay down her biggest mack to Vermaine as he told Cola sweet nothing he was indeed feeling her flow. Vermaine was loving every moment of their conversation still in shock that Cola had called him after four months. Cola talked sexy into the phone. "Mmmmm I'm not wearing anything" Vermaine dick got hard as he stroke his self as Cola talked nasty.

"Anyway boo" Cola said "I'll see you tomorrow in my tight jeans and five inch stiletto's". "Oh yeah baby" Vermaine replied back. Just from his response Cola knew everything would go as plan.

Cola yawned as she got up to head to Taylorland correctional center. She was in Colalicious mode once she had gotten herself together. She headed to 87th and the Dan Ryan so she could take the special bus that took family and friends to the prison. Cola didn't want her car no where near the prison just in case her plan back fired.

Bogus Azz Hood Chick/ PattiCake Taylor 250

"Name please" the driver asked Cola as she paid her fifty five dollars for a seat on the bus. "Cavika Warren" said Cola as she took her seat on the bus she couldn't wait to get to Taylorland.

After four hours the bus finally pulled up to the prison "thank god" Cola mumble, "damn bus kept overheating". Vermaine was all smiles as he watched Cola claim off the bus. Cola came in and didn't sign in she stayed behind and kick it with Vermaine in the lobby since no one was around.

"Muah" Cola kissed him so softly "so sorry babe I got to go but you will be seeing more of me trust me" Cola said. When Vermaine partner came to relieved him he told him Cola was okay to go in.

The inmate was already down from a visit Vermaine said.

As the officer check the call down sheet for inmates Cola hurried and sign in as Shavanika Stokes.

The bus driver told everyone he would be back in two hours. Cola had about an hour to put in plan in motion.

Bogus Azz Hood Chick/ PattiCake Taylor

Noon finally came back down to the visitor area. He was pissed he had to get research again for another visit and even more pissed because he told Cola to never pop up and that's what she had did.

Cola was smiling from ear to ear as Noon was snapping asking her why the fuck she up there and why the fuck she smiling, and he don't want no fucking visited from her he got a new bitch said Noon.

Cola continue to smiled "That's fine Noon I'm sorry that I didn't come last time I'm here now and I even brought you something". Noon began to smile now. "Here baby" Cola smiled so sweet.

Cola handed Noon fifteen small plastic bags. "I even found a way for you to sneak them back without you having to swallow them" said Cola. Cola pulled out some clear tape from her private area and began to tape the plastic bags into the palms of Noon hands and his fingertips. "Try not to close your hand too much so your hand want sweat and be easy on your pat down" Cola said still smiling.

Cola give Noon a big hug and kiss as the officers called for all riders of Tatum bus service "it time to go" the officer said.

Noon was smiling from ear to ear and so was Cola.

"I love you" Noon said, Cola blew Noon a kiss and walked out the visiting room.

Cola was tired and hungry from her long ass bus trip back home. She stopped at Margie's links and tips order her some food and was headed back to her crib for a nice bubble bath and a glass of wine.

As Cola returned home she ran into Devotion. They talked for a hot second before Devotion asked Cola to come watch the award show with her because she was bored.

Cola was glad she gotten that large tip and link combo. Cola and Devotion ate, drink and talk shit. Cola never knew she would have enjoyed herself with a youngster.

As Cola got up to the leave she promised Devotion they would kick it again soon. Cola couldn't wait to get in the crib soap and water was calling her name.

Cola bathed got comfortable and thought about Noon which she had not done since she left the visit.

A few days past and Cola decided to call Vermaine she thought his ass would have call her by now.

Ring, Ring!!
"Hello a woman said into the phone". "Hello may I speak to Vermaine" Cola said sweetly into the phone. 'Who's calling the woman asked". "It's Cola I'm just a friend". "Hold on baby, oh ok, I do see your name on his list of women" the woman replied. Cola started laughing "oh I'm on a list that's cute we just friends so it don't matter".

"Is he available or do I need to call back another time" Cola said in a pitchy voice. "I'm sorry baby" the lady said into the phone but Vermaine dead.

"WHAT"! Cola screamed as loud as she could "that's impossible". "Well honey I'm his momma and I've been to the hospital yesterday to identified his body and yes that's was my son Vermaine King David Smith". "I'm so sorry Ms. Smith.

"Thank you" Ms. Smith said into the phone. "May I ask how did he die Ms. Smith" Cola asked. "Baby" said Ms. Smith "all I know is seven inmates and three correctional officers died off rat poison".

Cola eyes got big as if her eyes were about to pop out her head. "I'm so sorry for your lost Ms. Smith" then Cola hung up.

The phone rang right back Cola didn't even look at the caller I.D. "Hello" said Cola! "You have a collect call from Taylorland correctional center inmate Kwame Woods". Cola hung up so quick she was scared out her mind. The phone rang again!

Cola knew the collect calls were recorded so it kinda ease her mind a little bit. The operator said press five to accept the collect called.

Cola push the five button to hear in the background "you killed my brother Kwame now I'm gonna kill you". Cola didn't know how to feel as she continue to listen. "NO"!!

Bogus Azz Hood Chick/ PattiCake Taylor 255

"PLEASE" Cola heard Noon say "she'll tell you she brought that shit up here not my soon to be baby momma Shavanika". "Man please don't kill her or me Cola did that shit".

"Cooooooooooola" she heard Noon say as he beg for his life "tell them please" was the last thing Cola heard before the phone went dead.

"Oh that bitch pregnant huh" Cola fussed out loud "I'm glad they think that hoe brought that rat poison mixed with heroin to the prison".

"Noon and Shavanika ass gonna be grass when them goons get done". Cola turned on the news to hear, here's the update at Taylorland correctional center.

"As of right now we have a total of nine inmates and three correctional officers died from a mixture of heroin and rat poison mix together". "Police is also investigating Kwame Woods who's the drug pin of Taylorland correctional center and is searching for his last visitor Shavanika Stokes if anyone knows the where abouts of Shavanika Stokes please contact

Bogus Azz Hood Chick/ PattiCake Taylor 256

your local police department" the news anchor said.

Cola decided she was gonna change her phone number just in case the prison looked at Noon phone list.

The next day... Cola went to get lunch as she was riding she saw a fat ass figured rolling up the street, she proceeded to pushed the pedal on her gas and laid on her horn and when Stuff turned around to see who was blowing he ran smack into the back of a cta bus on his motorcycle.

"Damn" Cola said "poor Stuff" then she drove away. Cola made a mental note as she laughed to contact Rosemary Young florist to send Stuff some flowers to his funeral.

When Cola got back home she changed her number ate her lunch then went to check her mail from the day before.

"Hey Cola" a female voice said out of no where.

Cola looked past the elevator. Cola rolled her eyes as she said what's up to Gold "how are you"? "I haven't seen you in a long time" said Cola.

"Yeah girl" Gold replied back "I been doing a lot of traveling since my sister death". "Why you didn't come to Silver funeral"? "I thought you all were so close" Gold said. "Sorry" Cola said "I had my own family emergency" she lied. "Plus I didn't get the flyer to the day of the funeral". "Anyway did the police find the killer of Silver and Starr"? Cola asked. "Nawl they still so call looking but I think I know who did it" Gold said.

"WHO"! Cola said with a crack in her voice.

"'Peanut" Gold said. "Who the hell is Peanut"? Cola said in a more confidence voice. "That guy who told Silver and I that Starr was dead I still think he had something to do with it" Gold replied, "I been dating him trying to see if I can find some clues or something". "Oh" Cola said with relief. "I hope the police find the killer" Cola said.

"Thanks" Gold said with a smile.

Cola smiled back and told Gold she would see her later. "You look good by the way" Cola added!

Gold did look good, she dye her hair black and even gain

Bogus Azz Hood Chick/ PattiCake Taylor

fifteen pounds she was thick like how Silver was. Ding Cola heard the elevator as she was checking the mailbox. "Colaaaaaaaa" Gold shouted! "What" Cola shouted back! "Are you getting on the elevator because it's here" Gold said sweetly. "Yeah" Cola ran before the door closed.

Cola stared at Gold as if she was her last supper. "Ummmm Gold can I ask you a question" said Cola. Cola couldn't help herself any longer. Cola took a deep breath and asked Gold to be her girlfriend.

"Wow" Cola said "I can't believe I'm attracted to a light skinned chick".

Gold huffed and puffed then she smacked the shit out of Cola. Gold called Cola every name in the book before walking off the elevator.

It was 11:00pm when Cola heard a knocked at her door. Cola looked through her peep hole and seen Gold standing there looking stupid. Cola finally opened the door and Gold jumped in Cola's arms and started kissing her.

Bogus Azz Hood Chick/ PattiCake Taylor 259

Cola kissed her back and Gold stayed all night. Cola was giving Gold the business and tried her new strap out too.

The next morning Gold turned over. "Mmmmm" Gold said "I have never had no fye sex like that before". Cola smiled "baby you ain't seen nothing yet" Cola replied. Gold lean over kissing Cola she asked Cola "do you want me to be your little secret because I ain't no dyke and I don't want people to think I'm one either".

Cola had a flash back to Wavon when he mention that same shit. Cola responded "hell nawl" now you can get the fuck out!

Cola put on her game face as she left the car rental place she was headed to Taylorland correctional center to check on Noon since he never called back. Cola began to worry. Cola didn't want to look like a suspect since she had miss a few visit. Cola was scared out her mind as she ask for Noon.

Cola was getting her lie together in her mind just in case she was question. Have a seat the officer told Cola. "I'm gonna go to the ladies room I'll be right back" said Cola. Cola sat on the toilet wondering what the officers was gonna tell her.

Cola exit the restroom and over heard someone ask for Kwame Woods. Cola froze in her spot as she heard the officers tell the girl she would have to talk to the warden.

"NiKysha Foxx" the officer said I need your I.D again. "NiKysha huh"! "who the fuck is this bitch" Cola mumble. Cola took a seat as she listen to the conversation of NiKysha and her friend.

"Yeah girl", NiKysha went on "I haven't heard from my nigga in over a week and the news keep talking about Noon being a drug pin and this bitch name Shavanika who visit him last".

As soon as Cola was about to approached this NiKysha hoe the officer called both of them back to the desk. "The warden busy but she told me to informed both of you to contact his mother and that Kwame couldn't have no visit today".

"Contact his momma I don't know her number" NiKysha

said.

Cola laughed out loud "girl fly, "who the fuck are you anyway to be up here visiting my man" said Cola. "Your man"? NiKysha said "bitch bye".

Cola just continued to laugh. "Officer Patterson can I talk to you a second I just want to know why I can't visit Kwame hell fuck that other bitch oops excuse my language" Cola said. "Cola now you know I'm not supposed to give out no information but Kwame on life support and he ain't gonna make it" replied Officer Patterson.

Cola went into a fake cry as she began to walked out the door to go to her rental car.

Nikysha just looked on wondering what the hell was going on. Cola gave NiKysha the middle finger as she drove off.

"Damn they must did a number on Noon" Cola mind wondered while she drove back home. "Well don't fuck with me and I want get you fuck up or fuck you up myself… BAM" Cola mumbled. Cola drove the rest of the way home in silence.

Bogus Azz Hood Chick/ PattiCake Taylor 262

Devotion was standing outside the building when Cola pulled up. Cola noticed Devotion had being crying. "What wrong girl" Cola asked? "Giiiiiiiirl" Devotion said "I think lost my job and to top it off my sugar daddy and I got caught by his wife".

"Your sugar daddy" Cola laughed to lighten the mood. "Well don't trip come on upstairs I'm about to cook the best chicken wings in Chicago" said Cola. Devotion laughed that sounds like a plan Cola.

Pow, pow, pow is all Cola and Devotion heard as they were about to entered the building. Cola turned around and saw blood every where.

Devotion was laid out on the ground. "OMG" Cola screamed as she saw a truck speed off. Cola grabbed Devotion purse hoping she had her cell phone. When Cola opened her purse all she saw was a stack of hundred dollars bills. Cola waited patiently to the ambulance came. It was too late Devotion was D. O. A.

Bogus Azz Hood Chick/ PattiCake Taylor 263

Cola was confused on what was going on and after the police asked one and a million questions. Cola headed to Devotion apartment to be nosy. Cola searched through Devotion crib like she was the police. Cola founded ten thousand under Devotion mattress. she couldn't believe her eyes as she continue to looked. Once Cola looked in Devotion purse she counted another five thousand and saw an I.D that said Monte with Devotion picture on it.

Cola snooped some more, when Cola was done it was clear that Devotion was a man.

Cola was on her way to her apartment as she tried to make sense of what just happen when she bumped into Gold.

"Gat damn it" Cola spat "this hoe would be using the stairs of all days". "Cola can I please talked to you for a second" Gold said with begging eyes. "Hell nawl" Cola snapped back "fuck I look like I ain't got shit to say to you". Cola continued to walked up the stairs.

Gold busted out "I know who killed my sister and cousin".

Bogus Azz Hood Chick/ PattiCake Taylor 264

Cola turned around so fast that she fall down a flight of stairs. "Cola are you okay" Gold ask trying not to laugh. "Yeah" Cola said kinda pissed "you just caught me off guard with that one". Cola heart beat fast as ever as she asked Gold who the killer was.

"It was Peanut he confessed girl" Gold replied back. "Peanut" Cola looked confused. "Yes they found his DNA on Starr and he just confused to both crimes" Gold said. "Wow" said Cola she was in shock. "Well I hope your family finds peace now talk to you later" Cola replied as she walked off.

Cola was frying her some chicken wings for dinner. She wanted to eat and take a bath so she could relaxed.

Cola looked at the clock "damn I shouldn't be eating at 10:00 at night". "Oh well" Cola mumble "let me see what the damn news talking about".

Cola was running her bath water when she heard the top story for tonight. "A pre-op transsexual who lived as a woman Devotion Louis was gunned down tonight by her lover wife after the wife caught her husband sucking Devotion private parts". "The police now have the woman in custody" the news anchor said.

Cola couldn't believe her ears. "Well thanks honey for the fifteen thousand dollars Devotion I sure did needed it" said Cola.

"I'm gonna get my ass up and go to Chitown Motor's and get me a better car in the morning" as Cola wrote in her journal. "After hearing Noon died from his beating and Shavanika was in prison". "I don't want nobody looking for me from my old car she mumble".

Cola exited the bus she was on ten she had cash and she knew she wouldn't have any problems getting a more up to date ride. Cola was looking at all the cars in parking lot smiling hard as ever as she went by everyone looking at the prices. A sales man finally walked up and ask Cola if she needed help. Cola turned around and piss on herself. "Mookie OMG of all people why I had to run into you".

Bogus Azz Hood Chick/ PattiCake Taylor 266

Cola took off running across the street happy it was a department store there. Cola bought her some new jeans, panties, soap and towel she went into the ladies room and freshen up when she was done she headed back to the bus stop pissed her day had been ruin.

As Cola waited for the bus Mookie came running across the street "Cola I'm so sorry" he said, "I never meant to hurt you this has been on my conscience for years". "I'm a grown man now I understand what I did to you was wrong can you please forgive me". "Please" Mookie said on bended knees.

Cola stood there with tears in her eyes "Mookie you know you was my first love and indeed you hurt me" replied Cola. "I'm sorry" Mookie said again.

"Give me a second and let me answer this call" Mookie said. "Yeah, yeah" Mookie said into his cell "let me call you back Tomorrow". Cola eyes got big as she yelled "Tomorrow"! "You still talk to that bitch" Cola yelled.

Mookie just stood there a moment before he said "yes she's

Bogus Azz Hood Chick/ PattiCake Taylor 267

my wife and we have five kids together four boys and one girl who we name Kola with a 'K' because for some reason she came out looking like you". Cola was in a dazed as she fell to her knees. Mookie picked Cola up and carried her into his job.

They entered his office he lock the door and then laid Cola on his sofa. Cola was crying so softly. Mookie began to wipe Cola tears as he started kissing her. "Cola" Mookie whispered "I'm sorry and I should have been with you I've missed you over the years you should have been my kids mother". "Nigga please" Cola said in between moans. "I love you Cola" Mookie kept saying over and over again.

As Mookie kissed Cola he was removing her pants hoping she wouldn't stop him.

Mookie went straight for Cola pussy after her third orgasm Cola sweetly call Mookie name.

"Mmmm yes baby" he said through his moans as he grind on Cola. Cola began to asked questions. "Do you love me"? "Do you love me more then Tomorrow stinky pussy ass"? Cola let out a giggled. "Yes Mookie" said as he entered Cola wet warm pussy. "I wish you was my wife I'm cuming" Mookie said with a grunt. "Yes baby" Cola moan back "cum all in this fye ass stuck pussy".

"Nahkomie" Mookie jumped up after hearing his government name.

"Nahkomie you dirty bastard I know you hear me calling you". Cola had eased Mookie cell phone from his waist when he was grinding on her and redial Tomorrow number. Mookie was so into what he was doing he never knew Tomorrow was on speaker phone. Tomorrow just listen through the whole process. "Nahkomie you fucking that bitch Cola after you talked about her like a dog over the years" Tomorrow cried.

"You a dumb bitch Tomorrow" Cola screamed back "you know nigga's be lying and you deaf knew Mookie wanted to fuck me". He made loved to me and ate my pussy at all. "Nahkomie you don't even eat my pussy what the fuck" Tomorrow began to cry harder.

Bogus Azz Hood Chick/ PattiCake Taylor 269

Mookie was heated at Cola. He grabbed her by her neck and threw her against the wall calling her all type of dirty bitches. "Let me go" Cola said through her chokes. "Let me go Mookie before your ass be in jail or meet your peace maker you decide" Cola tried to screamed.

Cola fixed her clothes and smiled. She walked out Mookie office walked up to the other sales man, told him she had cash he offered her the best car on the lot his old Lexus that he was trying to get rid of. Cola gave him ten thousand dollars and rolled off.

As Cola drove off all she could do was grin Mookie stood there mad as a pit bull. As Cola cruised the west side she decided to stop at the circle something she hadn't done in a long time. Cola wanted to hit the mall first she didn't want to be caught dead wearing the department store special's.

Cola rushed to the mall, so she could hurried and go to the circle it was Saturday and she knew all the nigga's would be out.

Bogus Azz Hood Chick/ PattiCake Taylor 270

Cola was gonna find her a thug she needed some dick.

Cola hit the Gucci store instead on Michigan avenue. She wasn't into all that fancy shit but she had a few thousands why not spend it. She step into the ladies room and re-freshen up something that she didn't do after having sex with Mookie. Cola jumped into her white on white Lexus and headed to the circle.

All eyes was on Cola as she exited her ride looking mighty good. She began to strut as if she was looking for someone.

"Hey miss lady" Cola heard this fine ass brother say. "Hey to you" Cola said. "What's good ma, what's your name"? " R O Y A L T Y" Cola said with a smile. "Yes indeed" he said back "you looking fine ma". "Your name should be Cola that names fit you to a tee". "Royalty with a cola coke body" he mumble. "Can a brother such as myself get to know you"? "Hell yeah" Cola was grinning from ear to ear now. "You ain't gonna tell me your name" Cola said through her smiles.

"Delight" he said. Cola began to laughed "that's not a good

name for no nigga".

"Well sweetie I'm not your typical nigga" Delight said. "Ugh, you a fag or something" Cola was now frown up. "nawl baby girl I am a woman"!

"Well damn" Cola said, "you the finest nigga I seen in a while, love your swag papi here's my number". "Holla at your new boo" Cola said the she strutted back to her car and drove off.

Cola spent a few days in the crib trying to figured what her next move was gonna be. Cola had spent those few days on the phone with Delight as well. Cola was questioning herself if she should just stop fucking with woman altogether.

Delight asked Cola to meet at her at the circle since she wouldn't let her come to her crib. Cola agreed after she shower she would come over. Cola got herself together she was looking good and smelling good she jumped in her Lexus and pumped the sounds of jack your body through the speakers so all eyes could be on her when she hit the circle. "Damn" Cola pumped in her seat "dude had to spend some money for this shit and all I give him was ten thousand".

Cola turned into the circle like she was the shit her music was bumping and all eyeballs was looking her way. Cola spotted Delight and some chick was all in her face going off. "Fuck you Delight" the chick said. Cola hurried and park her Lexus getting out wearing barely nothing making sure to switch harder the any hoe on the street.

"Deliiiiiiiiiight" Cola yelled as if she was at a concert so she could get the other female attention. "Oh this why you want me to leave because of this bitch" the female continue to yelled at Delight.

"I'll show this bitch" the female replied" before Cola knew it she had knocked old girl out for trying to run up on her.

Cola hugged and kissed Delight and told her to holla back. "I ain't got time for no drama" Cola said as she switched back to her car hearing cat calls.

As Cola cruise through the circle she seen yet another

familiar face "shit for Chicago to be such a huge place, I continue to see muther fuckers I hate" Cola said in anger.

"Yeah" Cola said "that's that muther fucker wondered what the fuck his ass doing on the west side". "Oh yeah nigga you beat me over a bitch" Cola said "through tears your ass is dead" Cola pushed her foot on that gas pedal as if she was in a race car and smack the shit out of Romance baby daddy.

He flew in the air before hitting the ground putting a huge dent in Cola Lexus. Cola speeded off hitting a few corners. Cola stopped at a station bought, her a container and filled it with gas got a rag and a lighter. Cola jumped back in her car went a few more block.

She began to wipe all her finger prints off everything she thought she may have touched with the gasoline.

Once Cola was done she poured the rest of the gasoline in the car before setting it on fire. Cola did her best to try and rushed home hoping no one saw her at all. She wasn't concerned with the Lexus because it was still in the owner's name. Cola never gotten the title switched over. The police would be looking for owner of the car not Cola.

"I gotta move" Cola said pacing her floor "I need to get out of Chicago before my ass in up in prison". "What the fuck where is my life headed". Well in the mean time I gotta get up off this west side" Cola continue to mumble.

Cola got in her hooptie car and headed to the store to get a newspaper she needed to find a place and fast. It took Cola almost an hour to get back home. The police and fire department had all the streets sewed up from the circle all the way to the Lexus that was on fire. Cola watched and did her best to listen to what people was saying then she decided just to head home before she got spotted.

Cola got up early after calling a few numbers the night before. She had a couple of appointments set up for apartment viewing. Cola went to looked at a few units on the south side.

Over the next couple days Cola packed so she could move. Cola ignored Delight calls scared that it might been a set up wasn't sure what she saw. Cola called the phone company to get her phone transfer over to her new place and changed her phone number. Cola left everything in her old apartment she filled her hooptie with all her clothes and shoes and whatever else could fit in.

  She headed to her new crib with all smiles she was able to pay up her rent three months with the last money she had. Cola would figure out along the way what she would do next she just needed to clear her mind she would worry about money later.

  Cola kept looking at her apartment very strange she was confused about the feeling then it hit her like a can of paint that she was in Peaches and Cream old apartment.

  Cola ran into the bedroom and looked under the hanger board shelf and indeed it was Peaches and Cream old unit. They all had wrote they names under the shelf saying friends forever the morning before hearing Cola name on the news.

  Those three months had flew by for Cola and she hadn't

found a job. She was all out of money and her rent for the fourth month was due. Cola was gonna go get her a trick to pay her bills.

She got dressed and was headed out the door she needed six hundred dollars and she needed it quick fast and in a hurry. Cola walked down her couple flights of stairs in her five inch heels as she was headed out there door Cola heard someone say "CHERRI"!

Cola turned around "hell nawl, you look ah mess" Cola said "Peaches what the hell happened to you" said Cola. You could tell Peaches had gotten hook on drugs. "Let me get five dollars" Peaches said.

Cola couldn't help but laughed "You use to be fine girl". "Well damn I can't get no hello" said Cola. "How are you before your ass start begging" Cola said. "I haven't seen you in how many years" said Cola.

Peaches became angry "you got five dollars or what" Peaches continue to say. "Yeah" Cola said "and it's my last but

I most deaf understand when you need a fix so here".

"Thanks girl" said Peaches!

Peaches was headed for the door. "Wait" Cola said "Where's Cream"? "Girl she dead nobody really know the cause but I think she had that package because she was out here just like me and she became very sick and died right up in our old apartment" Peaches said.

Cola gave Peaches a strange look. "You still stay in this building Peaches"? "Nawl, I moved out after Cream died". "I couldn't afford my rent" said Peaches. "These drugs got the best of me". "Oh okay" Cola said "well it was nice to see you" Cola turned around and headed back upstairs.

The next morning… Cola headed for the doctor for an appointment she haven't been in a while she knew she slept with a couple of the same men Cream and Peaches had slept with she needed to be sure she was fine.

After about a week of going crazy Cola was headed back to the doctor to get her results. The receptionist told Cola to have a seat that the doctor would be with her shortly.

As Cola was waiting she meet Tropical, she was waiting to see the doctor too. "Is Tropical your real name" Cola asked? "Yep" she said "my mom name me that because of this pigment disorder I have light here and dark there" said Tropical.

They exchanged a few more words before the receptionist called Cola. "Okay girl I'll call you later Tropical" said Cola. "No I wait for you Cola" Tropical replied.

Dr. Gupta went through Cola files and told her she was all clear of any disease. Cola jumped up and down happy as ever. Cola left and headed out to eat with Tropical.

Months had flew by…

Cola and Tropical became really good friends. Tropical even helped Cola on a few bills to get on her feet. Cola was at her last wits and didn't know what she was gonna do. Cola dig in her personal lock box until she came across what she was looking for.

Cola called Tropical and they talked for hours as they would do every night. "I'm so tired" Cola complain on the phone "this broke shit ain't hot".

"It okay friend" Tropical assured her.

"Easy for you to say you got a job" Cola spat back.

"Calm down Cola it ain't my fault is it anything I can do" Tropical said. Cola began to smiled "oh I'm glad you asked" Cola replied. Cola looked at the information she gotten out her lock box hoping they was still in business. "Can you drive to Mexico for me to get me some drugs" Cola asked? "WHAT Cola"!! "Why would you ask me some shit like that" Tropical spat! "Well forget it then" replied Cola "I thought you was my friend and was trying to help me out".

Tropical being excited that she had a friend she agreed to go. After they hung up for the night, Cola plan on calling the connects in Mexico. Tropical and Cola planned the trip for a couple of months.

The day had arrived and Tropical was scared out her mind. The plan was for Tropical to leave Friday night and return

Bogus Azz Hood Chick/ PattiCake Taylor 280

Monday night with no contact until she returned from Mexico. Cola was on ten she couldn't wait to get her products she planned on being the next big drug pin on the west side if all went as plan. Cola told Tropical to call the prepaid phone upon her arrival back. "DO NOT" Cola yelled through the phone call my house phone at any time. Cola wanted to be safe and have no contact if Tropical got busted.

Monday night had come and gone. Tuesday had come no word from Tropical yet. By the next Monday still no word from Tropical. Cola was going outta here mind and scared. Cola had sent Tropical to Mexico for drugs and something bad must have happen.

Cola gotten up and did what she thought was right she went to the police station and reported Tropical missing. Cola dressed in some oversize clothes a short wig and she cake on her makeup. Cola did not want to be recognize period.

"Next" the officer said! Cola stood there for a minute. "Step up" the fat white police officer said.

Bogus Azz Hood Chick/ PattiCake Taylor

"Yes I would like to report a friend missing" Cola said. "What her name" the officer said? "Tropical Fruit Juice Willis" said Cola! "What a ghetto name" the officer replied.

"What's your name young lady" the officer asked? "Ummmm" Cola said "my name is Monise". The officer hit a few things in the computer then told Cola to have a seat someone would be with her shortly.

Another officer came and escorted Cola to a room. Officer Chocolate was the name Cola have given him because he was fiiiiiine. He began to asked Cola a series of questions. Cola began to get choke up. "What's your relation to Tropical"? Officer Chocolate continue "She my friend" Cola said. "Just a friend" he said. "Yes sir" Cola replied back. "How long have you all been friends" the officer said? Cola was getting pissed off because the officer was asking the same damn question's as before.

"Sir we been friends a few months" said Cola. "What's a few months" he asked? "About six or seven months" Cola said in angry. "Can I go now" asked Cola. "NO"! officer Chocolate said in a high pitch voice. "Please tell me why I'm in here then when I just wanted to report a buddy missing" Cola spat . "Cola" he said. Cola looked at him confused.

"My name is Vanecha" Cola said. "Oh really" the officer replied back. "Yes really" Cola said in high pitch voice.

"Monise or Vanecha which one is it" officer Chocolate stated. "Both my first and middle is that a problem" Cola said Cola was happy she thought of that lie quick.

"Did you call a relative before coming to the station" he asked?

"No I don't know anybody in her family she just my buddy I really don't know her like that" Cola replied.

"We met at the doctor office and became cool that's it that's all geesh" said Cola . Cola was mad that she even came to the police station with all the questions the male officer was asking. "Sir I'm about to go you can't keep me you didn't read me my rights or nothing" said Cola. "Read you your rights huh you sure about that Cola" the officer replied. "Sir that's not my name" Cola replied. "Would you like a lawyer" he asked? "A lawyer for what I didn't do shit I been in this room going on five hours now and for what trying to report a dumb bitch" Cola spat. The officer looked at Cola sideways. "Hold tight" he said.

The next day…

Cola was glad that fight broke out in the lobby. The officer left Tropical files behind. Cola was in tears when she saw how they cut Tropical opened and stuff her with drugs to try and ship her back to the united states. Cola was grateful that it was Tropical and not her though.

Officer Chocolate appeared at Cola door.

Cola started to hate she name him officer Chocolate. Cola had this dumb look on her face pissed she didn't look through the peep hole first and wondered how in the hell the police knew where she stayed.

"How come" he started in with more question. "How come you talk to Tropical everyday but the weekend she was in

Bogus Azz Hood Chick/ PattiCake Taylor

Mexico" he asked?

"Sir" Cola began "does it even matter but to rest your mind I don't have long distance on my phone". "I'm done talking the next time you want to talk to me I'm gonna need a lawyer I feel like you harassing me now" said Cola. They both stood there at the door looking at it each other Cola was hoping he would just leave before she snapped the fuck out. he must have been reading her mind because as he turned around to leave. He informed her that he would be watching her and Tropical case would remain open. Cola looked at the officer with a I don't give two fucks look and slammed her door in his face.

FIVE YEARS LATER….

Cola was sitting on top of money A lawyer had contacted her a few years earlier to read the will of Nina Maria Dobson known as Climax.

After all Climax had left Cola two hundred and fifty thousands dollars. Climax had died. Cola wasn't sure how Climax died and she didn't ask any questions. Cola was just happy to see that check. Being that Cola had a unique name it wasn't hard to track her down. She was grateful for the lawyer hard work in finding her.

Cola finally had a game plan she was gonna use the money to open up her own night club called Tasteful Entertainment. She was happy it was gonna be a legit club and wasn't shit anybody could do to take that away from her. Cola needed to recruit some hot dancers for her club, her mind drafted off to a couple of people who would have been perfect. Mouthlicious and Gold, Cola wish Peaches was better and Cream was still here. "Damn" Cola said out loud. Mouthlicious was still good with her mouth word on the street she had herpes and although she could have been a money maker that would have been bad for business.

Poor Gold Cola shooked her head in disbelief Gold was killed by Peanut homeboy, Peanut founded out that Gold had lied on him and planted false evidence to get him life in prison for a crime he didn't commit.

Bogus Azz Hood Chick/ PattiCake Taylor 286

Things was getting crazy by the day Cola needed a reliable source of income she couldn't put her life in jeopardy anymore she had a son to think about: Nahkomie "Mookie" jr. He was going on five years old. Cola was trying to find the right time to locate Mookie, but she thought against it.

Cola went back to school she got a business degree she wanted to make sure things would be perfect when she opened up the hottest spot in "K" Town. Cola bought her a condo, a brand new car and she was excited.

It was Cola Krown Blue Royalty Johnson time to shine.

Six months later…

As Cola saw a packed club on her opening night at Tasteful Entertainment she spotted a few people she didn't like.

There was Jamal the nigga who gave her the STD and told the whole block they clown her for having a burning pussy. Pimp Don wanna be fine was in the house Cola would never forget he beat her in a coma. She watched both of them all night on her cctv camera from her purple rain theme office.

Bogus Azz Hood Chick/ PattiCake Taylor 287

As Cola was sitting in her office a thought came to her mind to treat them to a V.I.P when the club was over. "Just let that shit be" Cola mumble. Cola hired Yo-Yo Daddy B ex the light skinned bitch that jump her when Daddy B called her. Yo-Yo didn't even remember Cola and Cola thought that was perfect.

The night was finally over Cola thank everybody for her shit being a success. She was too happy. Cola didn't forget about the fellas and their V.I.P treatment. You know nigga's don't turned down no P.A.T, (Pussy Ass and Titties).

Cola had Yo-Yo to offer Jamal a blow job. Cola explained to Don wanna be fine she had some girls for him. All Cola wanted was thirty percent cut, he was down.
Cola paid Yo-Yo to go suck Jamal off in the V.I.P room...

Don wanna be fine was in Cola office to talk business. Cola excused herself to make sure her club was clear. The music was still flowing in air. Cola was feeling the beat of the music she laughed out loud as the D.J played the last song before he left. "The roof, the roof, the roof is on fire we don't need no water

Bogus Azz Hood Chick/ PattiCake Taylor

let this muther fucker burn" Cola snapped the fuck out right then.

She locked Jamal, Yo-Yo and Don wanna be fine inside the rooms they were in.

Opening night would be the last night of Tasteful Entertainment. Mr. Chocolate the police officer saw Cola set fire to her own club. After all these years Mr. Chocolate was still following Cola around trying to build a case for Tropical who turned out to be his daughter.

Mr. Chocolate called for backup as he arrested Cola. Cola was in the police car crying as she smelled badly of gasoline. All Cola could think of at that moment was her son all the money she invested in her club, her condo and her new life.

She knew her life would be over once the police found out there were three bodies left in her club. She began to talk to herself, "it's okay Cola one thing for sure I want be lonely in prison with all theose dyke bitches".

"Damn" Cola thought what a "**Bogus AZZ Hood Chick**".

Bogus Azz Hood Chick/ PattiCake Taylor 289

THE END!! Sincerely, Ms. PattiCake Taylor Author of

Bogus AZZ Hood Chick!!

"13095319" Cola kept saying to herself she couldn't believe she was sitting in prison two years already.

"WHAT THE FUCK"!

Bogus AZZ Hood Chick Behind Bars © 2013 by: PattiCake Taylor coming soon!!

Turn Over >>>>>>>>>>>>>>>>>

Bogus Azz Hood Chick/ PattiCake Taylor

Special shout outs: to my Pre-Orders before my re-submission of my Proof copy!! Thank You 4 believing in ME!! BAM!!

Aye Neloms

Jay Cee Cade

Crystal S.

Bria S.

Jane Doe

J.R. Young

Katrina B.

Beverly P.

EBay

Whoppa

Nellie T.

Dannie/Momma Seals/ Fashionable Addictions

Toy M.

Chyna @ E's Studio

Chocolate "Hair Stylist"

Tina H.

Bogus Azz Hood Chick/ PattiCake Taylor

Sallie Y.

Monisha H./Luscious Boutique

Queen Sunshine/Chicago Chix's Viritual Boutique

DSW

Janise T.

Renita Y.

Jeanette

Shiann

Nick J.

Danielle W.

John E.

Tamika H.

Bogus Azz Hood Chick/ PattiCake Taylor

Pa Pow Boom Kack Productions: Presents A taste of
POETRY!

(all Poetry printed as given)

<u>I'm not A Poet</u>

She's a

Writer

No

She's a

Poet

No

She's a fighter

No

She's a

Lover

NO

Im neither or

Im a woman that is torn

And

Scorned

Choosing

Paper and pen

To describe

The feelings of emotion

Within

Because inside

is my home

And I sit alone

Like

Macaulay Culkin

Wishing

That you would stop

Reading the words that I write

And search in between the lines

That defines

How many times

Ive

Died to live

But

The question is:

Who dares to dive?

Dive into

The life

Of a woman

Whose memories

Are filled with attempts

Of suicide

Because you

Refuse to move aside

To allow love to reside inside of me

And I cant call it history

Because the memory of love

Missed me

So I hide.

But knowing

That im only

Two blocks from heaven

And across the street from God

I nod

Remembering that death

Has no turn around

Or turn about

so I don't say good-bye

as I reach flat line

my soul

Screams at me

Take your hand off the knob

And I do

I reach for the phonebook

To call just to feel close to you

And beside heaven

It reads:

You have a second chance

So I yell

If that so true

In this second chance will

I be mad man, never felt comfortable

As a woman,

Will mommy love me,

Cause she let daddy push up on me,

Will the devil push hisself down

Cause im tired of laying on the ground?

See

Im not a writer

Im not a poet

Nor the above thee

im a survivor of thee

im not a writer

im not a poet

a poet just writes to me!

By Wise from ATL ©

Bogus Azz Hood Chick/ PattiCake Taylor

<u>One hand on my breast</u>

one hand on my breast

the other hand grab her dreads

as I laid on the bed with spreaded legs..

relaxed in a way only she can get me. no pillow to prop my head no towels

for the bed

that I was wetting up

even though she caught every drop as she licked from the bottom up!

This is how I wanted it and thats how she gave it...

She made me feel like she's the only one that can fuck me and put me in a daze..

Change my whole world

Then I began to rearrange and

 a few hours later she had me thinking bout

Something!

Like, I gotta have it again and

My legs went numb from being in the air..

But I enjoyed it.

I liked the way she lick me from the bottom up

My thick thighs

And fat ass

Shit she cant get enuff.

and I thought she had me sprung

And all along its her that wants more

She's hungry and i gotta feed her.

So with one hand on my breast

And the other grabbing her dreads

I'm gonna make sure she eats

And gets full.

I'm gonna wrap my legs around her neck

Make her suck my pussy and take her tongue and flick my clit!

And she knows im submissive

So she'll tell me to suck her dick

And if u dont know its the one she straps on and it never goes limp

I mean she gets it in

And I love it

And while she's in it....I'll sing a melody of yes's

And with one hand on my breast

And the other grabbing her dreads

This moment right here,

I never want to end...

Lyrical Flamezzz (Mackya Curry) of Chicago © 2013

Bogus Azz Hood Chick/ PattiCake Taylor

Wow! Ladies it has happened to me, yes to me, getting burned to the 3rd degree

Been down that road, I love you, You're my everything, I would never do you wrong, Never put my hands on

you........ That shit wasnt true

Lies lies LIES!

How about the F***ing truth sometimes

Oh yea thats right, You were never mine

Strung me along making me feel like I was your Prize

With all your Mistreatings, Cheatings and Beatings

You had become my greatest demise..... for a while

Tried to steal All of my joy, All of my strength, Keeping me at bay from my family

Why in the hell would you want to do this to me, I never deserved that

Now i'm not one of those females that lives in the past

But the wrongs have left scars that last

Imprints on my life that i will Never forget

Still to this day makes me question, Will I ever feel like the same ole me again

The answer is No, She died back with all the lies (I love you), Beatings (Him Her Them), Mistreating

(Everthing bad) that derived

And grown from that Naive catapillar into the beautiful Black Butterfly, that I was put on this earth to be

God has funny way of showing you just what you need.

Can't be found in Anyone or Anything, But me.

30 yrs later I've learned to know my past is just that, my past, Those relationships weren't meant to last

but to prepare me for the road that you have prepared for me

4 kids, A house, A business to run

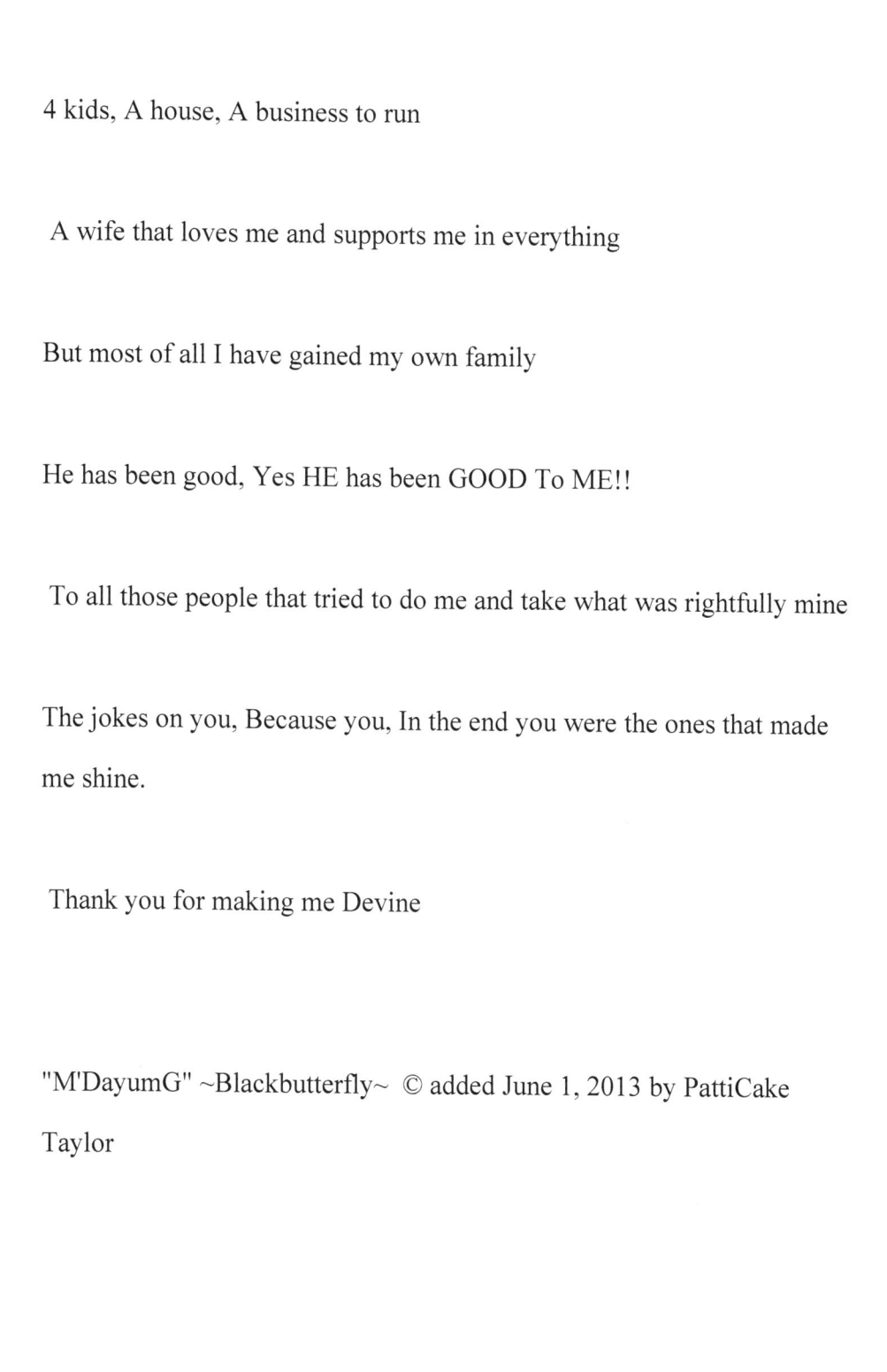

A wife that loves me and supports me in everything

But most of all I have gained my own family

He has been good, Yes HE has been GOOD To ME!!

To all those people that tried to do me and take what was rightfully mine

The jokes on you, Because you, In the end you were the ones that made me shine.

Thank you for making me Devine

"M'DayumG" ~Blackbutterfly~ © added June 1, 2013 by PattiCake Taylor

TURN OVER >>>>>>>>>>>>>>>>

LIES OF A CONVICT

PattiCake Taylor

Paragraphs of Lies
By: PattiCake Taylor

Bogus AZZ Hood Chick

By: PattiCake Taylor

Made in the USA
Charleston, SC
04 May 2015